Gloria Morgan has been writing since she was ten. She grew up in London but now lives half way up the M1, on the left. Her favourite colour is red and her favourite day is Thursday. She's had various jobs in offices, colleges, hospitals and photographic studios while the stories and plays have just kept coming. She enjoys travelling and some of the interesting people and places she's seen have found their way into her books. Best of all, Gloria likes to write for young readers. She spends most of her time at her computer bashing away at her latest manuscript. When she drags herself away from the screen she enjoys pottering in her garden and going for long walks, preferably with a dog. To find out what she's working on now visit her website: www.callie-cobooks.co.uk

By the same author:

Kinmers Lea
Dream Me Home

For slightly younger readers:

Shan and the Tree
Shan and the Snow
Shan and the Pond

The Ducking Stool

Gloria Morgan

A CIP catalogue record for this title is available from the British Library

ISBN 978-184426-730-9

First published in 2009 by
Callie-Co Books, Nottingham

www.callie-cobooks.co.uk

Printed and bound by print-on-demand-worldwide.com

The Ducking Stool

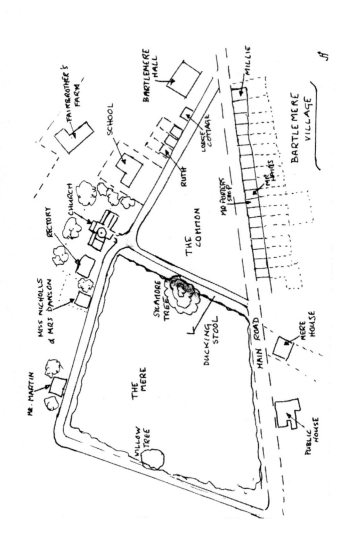

MR. MARTIN

MISS NICHOLS
& MRS DAWSON

RECTORY

CHURCH

SCHOOL

FAIRBROTHER'S
FARM

BARTLEMERE
HALL

LOUISE'S
COTTAGE

RUTH

THE COMMON

MR PORTER'S
SHOP

THE
HINDS

MILLIE

BARTLEMERE
VILLAGE

SYCAMORE
TREE

DUCKING
STOOL

THE MERE

WILLOW
TREE

MAIN ROAD

MERE
HOUSE

PUBLIC
HOUSE

CHAPTER 1

It was twenty to nine on Monday morning the 26th of June 1944. Ten-year-old Megan Michaels sat at the breakfast table opposite her elder brother, John. A pile of buttered toast was getting cold on its plate next to a big, brown, china tea pot. Neither of the children had eaten a thing.

Mrs Pleeth, their guardian, sat anxiously between them at the end of the table. She shook her head helplessly. She sighed and got up from her place and went into the kitchen.

Megan continued to stare silently at the red chequered tablecloth. Her brother's hands lay limply in his lap and he was studying them intently.

The sun was pouring in through the big windows and sparkling on the cut glass salt and pepper pots.

The uncomfortable silence was broken by a sharp rap on the front door.

Mr Pleeth, seated at the other end of the table, got to his feet and reached for his helmet – his badge of office as village constable. A knock at the front door always signalled police business. All other visitors came round to the back.

He put his helmet on and lifted his tunic off the back of the chair. He slid his arms into it, buttoning it up as he left the room. They heard him open the front door.

After a few muffled words of conversation, Mr Pleeth returned to the breakfast room. He sat down heavily, removing his helmet and setting it carefully on one side. Then he reached out across the table for his big, thick, 'Incident Book' and drew it towards him.

He flicked through the lined pages, full of carefully written paragraphs, each neatly ruled off, until he came to the next available space to make an entry.

He took up a fountain pen lying near his plate, unscrewed the top and shook it a couple of times until he saw a bead of ink appear on the nib.

Mrs Pleeth came back from the kitchen.

"Not more trouble, Walter?"

Mr Pleeth shook his head.

"It's nothing much. School's closed this morning, that's all. Miss Nicholls' mother has taken poorly and she has to stay at home and look after her. She says she'll open up at one o'clock. I'll notify people."

Mrs Pleeth looked relieved and turned to the children.

"Well, then, there's no hurry to have your breakfast, is there? Megan, why don't you go back up to your room, dear? John, you go with her and keep her company. I'll make a fresh pot of tea and some more toast and bring you up a tray in case you find your appetite later."

"Thank you," John muttered.

Megan watched Mr Pleeth's pen as it scratched across the coarse paper. He was making his second entry of the day.

The first entry, made an hour ago, read: "Body of drowned man discovered floating in The Mere."

CHAPTER 2

Mr Pleeth's first entry of the day continued:

"Body observed from the front bedroom window of Mere House by Miss Megan Michaels, evacuee from London, staying at the home of Mr & Mrs Walter Pleeth. Constable Pleeth attended the scene and identified the dead man as Cyril Roseby, aged 33, former soldier, lodging with Eustace Hains (retired carpenter) at Forge Cottage. The dead man appeared to have fallen into the water after climbing up on the ducking stool. Body retrieved and lodged temporarily in an out-building at Mere House. Urgent message telephoned to the doctor in Market Hampton."

Back upstairs in her room, Megan sat on the edge of the bed and tried to blot out the gruesome picture of the drowned man, which seemed to be stuck permanently in front of her eyes, whether they were open or closed.

Four years ago, to escape from the London Blitz, Megan and John had stayed for eight months at Mere House, in Bartlemere village. All through that first visit the tall shape of the ducking stool had dominated the landscape.

The structure was still there, sticking up at an angle across the dark water of The Mere like half a giant letter X. On the end above the water there was a crude seat, while the other end was weighted down and fixed to the ground.

The moment she had drawn back her bedroom curtains this morning and looked out across the front garden of Mere House, Megan had known something was wrong.

Today, the angle of the ducking stool was reversed. It was like seeing a see-saw, tilted the other way. The weighted end was sticking up in the air with the seat end under the water and what looked like a big bundle floating beside it. When Megan had looked more closely she'd realised the bundle was the shape of a person.

Then she had screamed. Her brother had been the first to respond. The door to his room was next to hers – he slept at the back of the house. In an instant he had dashed to her side. As she pointed dumbly through the window, he had taken a long look and confirmed for himself what she had seen.

As Mrs Pleeth came panting up the stairs from the kitchen, John was already leading Megan away from the window. As soon as Mrs Pleeth had looked out and seen what had caused Megan's alarm, she hurried back down the stairs to tell her husband.

Mr Pleeth went outside immediately to investigate.

Megan had gone with John into his room. She heard Mrs Pleeth come back upstairs and go and close the front curtains again.

Mrs Pleeth had tried very hard to keep everything as normal as possible. She had insisted the children get washed and dressed and come down for their breakfast. There was nothing for them to worry about, she said. It was too bad that such a horrible accident should have happened right outside their house. Mr Pleeth would deal with all the necessary business after they had gone to school. The one and only telephone in the village was kept on Mr Pleeth's desk, to be used in case of emergency.

Megan was too shocked to cry. She didn't even want to speak. She couldn't think. She didn't know what she wanted, except to be left alone until the awful knotted feeling in her throat went away.

Gradually it eased, and she felt calmer. But then the thoughts came crowding into her head, so many and so fast that she didn't know what to think first. Her head began to spin, with so many thoughts all hammering at her at once.

When the message came that they were excused school for the morning, she was so relieved.

She couldn't have coped with going, although she had looked forward to it so much. She had wanted to run back to the little old school across The Common and meet all her friends again, and talk and laugh and sit with them and do their lessons together.

She had wanted to see Miss Nicholls again, too. Her dear Miss Nicholls, who had been her most favourite teacher ever in the whole world. Today was going to be such a good day.

But now, this. What a terrible start to her first week back at school in Bartlemere.

The bedroom door opened and someone came in.

"You all right?" It was her brother. Megan looked up and nodded.

"Listen, Meg, I've got to go. Did you remember I'm not going to school? I've got to go up to the farm and see Mr Fairbrother at nine o'clock about starting work."

Meg stared at him. She'd forgotten he wouldn't be coming to school with her. She still couldn't find anything to say.

"Will you be all right? 'Cos I'll stop here if you need me. Only it's nearly nine and if I'm going, I should leave or I'll be late."

"You go, John. I'm okay. Honest."

"Good for you, Meg. Look – don't let this get you down." He gave her a quick hug. "I must dash." He helped himself to a piece of toast as he passed the tray. "Meg, you really should eat some of this. It's a terrible waste of food, you know."

"Mrs Pleeth'll give it to the chickens."

"Chickens should eat chicken food, not our food. There's not enough of it about to waste any, even in the country. We'd never throw good food away at home."

He brought her over a slice of toast, thick and well browned and generously buttered.

"Come on, that's half your butter ration for the week spread on there, so eat up."

He stood over her until she started to nibble at it. He nodded approval, ruffled up her hair, and went quickly out of the door and down the stairs. Moments later she heard the back door bang behind him.

She wondered how he was feeling about going to work at the farm. She knew he would rather be studying. He had made a flying start at the boys' grammar school back home. His great ambition was to be a scientist. But he had turned fourteen now and that was the leaving age when you attended a village school like Bartlemere.

Yesterday, Mr Pleeth had taken John into the front room, which served as the Constable's Office, to explain the situation to him. John had reported their conversation to Meg afterwards.

"Every able-bodied chap has to do his bit for the war effort," Mr Pleeth had told him. "All the farm labourers have been called up into the army. You're not old enough for that yet, but this is your chance to serve your country and you should be proud to do it. You're a strong lad and you'll be a good help up at the farm, especially come harvest time."

Meg remembered Mr Fairbrother, the farmer. His daughter, Kathleen, had been Megan's friend and classmate. She hoped Mr Fairbrother would keep an eye on her brother.

Meg finished her toast and lay down again on her bed. The faded, pink-patterned bedroom curtains moved slightly in the breeze from the open window. Megan saw them through half-closed eyes. Her thoughts went back to the weekend.

There was so much going on in her life and it was all happening too quickly. She needed to clear her head.

Only two days ago she had woken up in her own bed at home. Yesterday, Mummy had been with her when she woke here in Mere House. Today, she had woken all on her own and seen a dead body outside the window.

CHAPTER 3

Megan remembered Saturday the 24th of June as a day of queues.

They had packed their suitcases the night before.

The previous week, bombing raids had begun again in earnest in the part of South London where they lived.

"Megan, you can only take what you need. You're putting far too much in your case. You'll have to take some of those things out."

"But Mummy, I need to take it all."

"No, you don't. You want to take it all. That isn't the same thing. You can only take what you really need."

Megan felt angry and helpless. Tears were not far away when her mother looked over what she had packed and insisted some favourite things had to be left behind.

"You must be able to carry your case yourself, Megan. Taking those extra things out will have made it lighter." As her mother closed the lid, Megan couldn't help crying.

"I don't want to go at all."

"I know you don't, darling. But it's too dangerous for you to stay here."

None of them wanted to make this journey. Worst of all was knowing that when they got to Bartlemere, she and John would stay and their mother would come back to London without them.

Their mother had got them up early on Saturday morning.

When they set out to walk to their local railway station Megan's case felt as heavy as lead. She struggled to lift it, despite leaving so many things behind. The weight of the case made her drag her feet.

Megan could remember a day out with John to the station to collect engine numbers. John liked to take sandwiches and a bottle of pop, and find a safe place at the far end of the platform where he could sit and write down the engine numbers in his notebook as he spotted each train coming in. She remembered how thrilled she had been when John agreed to take her with him. That had been an exciting day. Sometimes the driver had waved and blown his whistle for them. Today was quite different.

At the station the signboard giving the time of the next train wasn't working. The platform was packed with bad-tempered people. After a long wait they caught a local train for the half-hour journey into the centre of London.

When they got off they joined a queue, along with dozens of other people, for a bus to Liverpool Street Station, the main railway terminus from where their train to Market Hampton departed.

At Liverpool Street Station they couldn't believe the crowds. It seemed everyone in London wanted to leave.

They had to join more queues of people waiting to buy tickets and then had to queue again to get on the train.

There was an endless wait before they were able to get on the platform. Hundreds of people wanted to travel, everyone pushing and shoving towards the barrier. When the man finally opened the gates, the crowd surged forward and Megan clung to John's hand, afraid of getting separated in the crush.

They followed their mother the whole length of the train and back, but couldn't find anywhere to sit. Some people were actually fighting to get to a place. The last coach was the guard's van and they could see through the tiny windows that it was already crammed full.

Mummy was about to turn away when the door opened and hands reached down to them. They climbed aboard, up a steep step. Megan heaved her suitcase up behind her. Everyone inside pressed closer together so they were able to squeeze in. There were no seats. Megan sat on their luggage while Mummy and John stood. They were squashed in like sardines. There was almost no ventilation, no refreshments, no toilet.

Six hours later they finally got off at Market Hampton. It was bliss to climb down from the train and stretch their legs.

"Our first job is to find the public conveniences," Mother said, as she handed them each a penny.

"There's a sign," John pointed. "Near the ticket office."

"I asked Mrs Pleeth to have a word with Mr Fairbrother," Mother said as they came out into the sunshine a few minutes later, "so I'm hoping someone has come to pick us up."

Sure enough, one of the older lads from the farm was waiting for them in the station forecourt with a pony and trap. He helped them climb up into a little open carriage and settle themselves on the bench seats. John and Megan sat on one side, their mother facing them, their luggage piled round their feet.

"Isn't it lovely to get some fresh air?" Mother said, as the trap sped along.

"How long will it take to get there?" Megan wondered.

"About half an hour."

When they arrived, Mere House was exactly as Megan remembered it. She couldn't believe she hadn't seen it for nearly four years.

Mr and Mrs Pleeth made them very welcome.

The table was laid and tea was waiting for them – ham and eggs, home-made pickles, bread and butter, jam and a fruit trifle. So much food looked like a feast to Megan and her family.

Half-a-dozen eggs was the ration for all three of them for a fortnight. Mrs Pleeth's hens laid more than that every day. Although food rationing was in force everywhere, people who lived in the country had a lot of extras that Londoners never saw.

"I can't imagine how you make one ounce of cheese each and two ounces of jam last for a whole week," Mrs Pleeth told their mother later, as she cleared the table.

"Well, that's what we have to do, and that's when there's any jam in the shops to buy. Often there isn't."

"We don't know how well off we are in the country," Mrs Pleeth nodded. "One thing you can be sure of – these two will be well fed while they're with us."

CHAPTER 4

After tea, Mother said: "I think we three could do with a walk. Let's stroll round The Common and see what's changed since we were last here."

The Common was a big expanse of grass, roughly shaped like a triangle, with a broad gravel path along all three sides. It took about twenty minutes to walk all the way round. Since olden days the villagers had grazed their animals here. Now, as well as a few sheep who kept the grass down, it was a favourite playground for the local children.

As they came out of the gate of Mere House they met a familiar figure coming towards them. John and Megan ran up to him:

"Mr Martin! Hello!"

"Bless my soul – if it isn't you two young bundles of trouble. Come back to plague the life out us again, have you?" Mr Martin laughed loudly. "Good evening, to you, Mrs Michaels. Nice to see you again. These two are growing!"

"Hello, Mr Martin. Yes, they're bigger than you remember them, aren't they? John's fourteen now and Megan's nearly eleven."

"Are you back to stay?"

"I'm not, but the children are."

"Because of the doodlebugs, I suppose?"

"That's right. They're causing havoc in London. I'll feel better knowing these two are well out of harm's way. But, of course, I shall miss them terribly. But I have a job I must go back to."

"Well, we'll keep an eye on them. You pop round and see me, young John. I've a few things in my yard I can show you. Some pieces of shrapnel you'd be interested in, no doubt. You come any time you like."

"Thank you, Mr Martin." John liked Mr Martin.

"And you, me darlin'." Mr Martin beamed at Megan.

"Thank you." Megan smiled back. She liked Mr Martin, too. He was always laughing. Sometimes he'd sing out loud, at the top of his voice. He never cared what people thought. The people in the village said he was a gipsy, but he'd lived there all his life so she could never make sense of that. His home was a kind of permanent scrap yard, full of broken down farm machinery, motor parts, and all kinds of metal bits and pieces. John loved to go and poke around there.

"Well, I'll be on my way. Good evening to you, again." Megan laughed as he raised his hat and bowed to their mother and went off, almost dancing along.

"He'll be on his way to get his pint at The Man in the Moon, no doubt," Mother said, "so in no time at all I expect the whole place will know you're back."

The village pub, The Man in the Moon, was next door to Mere House, to the left.

Megan, John and their mother turned right and strolled down the part of the gravel path that followed the main road through the village. This was where most people in the village lived, in their neat cottages that looked out over The Common.

Everything seemed very much as they remembered it. Well-tended gardens, warm red bricks, weathered thatch and tiles, small square window panes.

They paused at the village shop.

"I don't think they've changed the window display since we left!" John laughed.

A little further along they saw Mr Hains, sitting outside his cottage door.

"Evening, Mr Hains. Just catching the last of the sunshine?" Mother called to him.

"I am at that. Good evening to you. Coming back again to stay, then?"

"The children are."

"Oh, aye."

"He can be a grumpy old thing," Megan muttered to her mother as they walked on.

Immediately ahead of them was the gable-end of Bartlemere Hall, a large mansion that in its heyday had been a very grand affair but was now shut up and empty.

Here the path turned off the main road at a sharp angle. They followed it up the other side of The Common, past the Lodge Gate cottage of Bartlemere Hall.

Megan ran ahead, towards the village school. She stood and looked lovingly at the quaint little building. It was the smallest school Megan had ever seen. There was just one classroom, where all the children were taught together. Megan couldn't wait to rejoin her old school friends for the few remaining weeks of the summer term.

Megan's mother caught up with her. She looked around and pointed out a notice pinned to the school door.

"Look, they're putting on a play. That sounds fun."

14

"When is it?"

Mummy scanned the poster more closely.

"It's on Saturday the 8th of July and it's 'The Rivals'. Oh, that's a good one."

"Do you know it, Mummy?"

"Yes, I do. In fact, a very long time ago, when I was at school, I took part in a production of it."

"Did you? Tell me!" Megan hopped up and down with excitement.

"What's it about?" John wanted to know.

"It's a comedy. It's all about mistaken identity and people not being who they say they are. And there's an old lady in it who's a real snob. She tries to pretend she's very well educated so she uses lots of long words, but she always gets the meaning wrong and makes a complete fool of herself."

"What part did you play?"

The children were fascinated. This was something new about their mother that they hadn't known before. She was an actress!

"I played Lucy, the maid."

"Is she the heroine?" Megan wanted to know.

"No, she isn't. The heroine is Lydia Languish. But I enjoyed playing Lucy. She's a very naughty girl. The other characters pay Lucy to carry messages for them but she often delivers a different message from what they said. She stirs up a lot of trouble and, of course, she keeps all the money."

Mummy was laughing at the memory of it. She had enjoyed it so much, when she was a girl.

Suddenly they heard raised voices from inside the school building, a man and a woman.

"I don't know what you're talking about!"

Megan stiffened.

"That's Miss Nicholls. She doesn't usually sound like that. She was practically shouting."

"Hush and listen a minute." Mummy caught hold of Megan's hand. "I think they must be having a rehearsal."

A man's voice spoke:

"Oh, I think you do, my dear."

His voice was not loud but it had an edge to it. Megan was shocked at his tone. It sounded truly threatening. She tried to put a name to the voice, but couldn't.

The man spoke again, louder this time.

"I know all about you and Beverley. Don't think you can keep that a secret from me!"

Miss Nicholls' only reply was a kind of squeak.

"Do you think she's forgotten her lines?" John suggested.

"I think they both have," Mummy replied. "I don't remember a scene like that from the production I was in. Come along."

She linked arms with both of them and together they strolled on up the gravel path, past the entrance to the farm and then on to the church.

The mellow old stone glowed golden in the late evening sunshine. By the lych-gate, two tall yew trees cast black shadows.

The Rectory was next door to the church, and beyond that the cottage where Miss Nicholls lived with her mother, Mrs Danson. Their only other neighbour was Mr Martin. You couldn't see his untidy junkyard from the path.

Here, they turned sharply again, following the angle of the Common. Directly ahead was Mere House. To their right, taking up most of the space on that side of The Common, was The Mere that gave the house its name.

The expanse of deep, dark water was too big to be called a pond but not large enough to be a lake. The clusters of reeds jutting through the surface made it unsafe for swimming. Although it was not fenced off, all the local children kept away from it. It seemed gloomy and chilly on even the warmest day.

Around the banks there were some straggly bushes and a few trees. Two ducks sitting on the grass at the brink got up and waddled away as they walked by.

Sticking out at an angle over the water was the familiar sight of the ducking stool.

Nearly fifty years ago, Bartlemere had held an historic pageant to mark the turn of the century from 1899 to 1900. There had been a maypole and a set of stocks and an elaborate pavilion, but over the years they had all disappeared. The ducking stool was the only thing left.

"Fancy that still being here," Mummy remarked, as they passed.

Megan yawned.

"Are you about ready for bed, darling?" Mummy asked, "Because I am."

"Yes."

"Me, too," John agreed.

"So it's early nights all round, yes?"

The children nodded agreement as they went back in through the gate and round to the back door of Mere House.

CHAPTER 5

Very late at night on that Saturday, Megan had woken up to the sound of loud voices.

Men were shouting. She felt confused. What was going on? Where was she?

She was sure she was not at home, but the room was in total darkness and she couldn't get her bearings. Then she remembered she was in the front bedroom at Mere House.

Her mother had come up to put her to bed as soon as they came in from their walk. When Megan was settled down and comfortable, her mother kissed her goodnight. She told her she was going in to check on John and then go back downstairs to join Mrs Pleeth for a cup of tea before coming up herself.

Megan was sleeping on a camp bed. Tomorrow, she would move into the big bed, where her mother was sleeping tonight.

Her mother must have pulled the blackout blinds shut when she came up to bed.

Megan listened to the voices. Now one of the men was singing. She heard her mother turning over in the big bed next to hers.

"You awake, Mummy?"

"Yes, darling. Are you?"

"Yes. What's that shouting?"

"I don't know. Shall we peep out and see?"

They both slipped out of bed and Mummy pulled an inch of the blackout blind aside. They hadn't put the light on in their bedroom so they weren't breaking the law. As village constable, Mr Pleeth was very particular about not showing lights in the house at night.

Peering out, Megan could see a man up on the ducking stool. He had climbed right to the top and was sitting in the seat. There was a little railing, like an armrest, round the end, but nothing else to stop him plunging into the water.

He had a bottle of beer in his hand. He kept taking a swig. When he wasn't drinking from it, he was waving it about and yelling.

Mr Pleeth, in his uniform jacket and police helmet, stood at the water's edge.

"Be quiet, Roseby! Don't make me have to tell you again. You'll wake half the village with this noise."

The man's response was to pretend to strum his beer bottle like a ukulele. He threw back his head a roared:

"I'm a window cleaner! Look at little me. When I'm cleaning windows you'd be amazed at what I see!"

"Roseby! Come down from there this minute!"

"I'm waiting by a lamp-post for a lady to go past. What I know about her would really make you gasp!"

"I'm warning you, Roseby. Get down here now!"

"And just what are you going to do if I don't?"

"As Parish Constable I have the power to lock you up, you know that, don't you?"

"Ooooh! Mr Pleeth the pleethman is going to lock me up and throw away the key! But first, you've got to catch me, haven't you? Anyone for tennis, old chums?"

With that, he hurled his empty beer bottle into the air and batted it into The Mere with his fist, as though he was serving a tennis ball.

Mr Pleeth was standing with his back to the bedroom window, stiff with rage.

Megan giggled.

"How will he make him get down, Mummy?"

"I don't know, darling, but I think it might take quite a long time. We should go back to bed and let Mr Pleeth sort it out."

She closed the blackout blind and turned away from the window.

Megan wondered who the man was. She'd never seen him before.

"That man didn't live in the village when we were here before, did he Mummy?"

"I don't remember him."

"Neither do I."

Most people made a point of not upsetting Mr Pleeth. Megan certainly tried not to. But this Mr Roseby didn't seem to be at all bothered. It was really funny, watching Mr Pleeth get so cross.

Megan didn't want to go back to her camp bed.

"Can I get in with you, Mummy?"

"Yes, of course. Come on."

It was so good to snuggle up. Mummy stroked Megan's hair and kissed her forehead.

Megan let herself be swallowed up in a lovely cuddle until she forgot the commotion outside. She wanted to make the most of this one chance to enjoy precious hugs and kisses and falling asleep together. She couldn't bear to think that tomorrow Mummy would go home and she would have to stay in Bartlemere without her.

CHAPTER 6

When Megan and her mother came down to breakfast on Sunday morning 25th June, Mr Pleeth was already at the table, in shirtsleeves and braces. His face was like a thundercloud. John was sitting quietly alongside him. Mrs Pleeth was busy in the kitchen.

John got up when they came in and gave each of them a hug. Then he went back to his place and Megan and Mummy sat down opposite him.

Mr Pleeth didn't move or speak. Mummy ignored his grumpy face.

"Good morning, Mr Pleeth! How are you this morning?"

Mr Pleeth only nodded in response.

"You had a disturbed night last night, didn't you? Who was that man making such a silly fuss outside the house?"

"He's nothing but an ignorant troublemaker."

"What fuss? What was going on, Meg?" John's curiosity was aroused.

"There was this man outside, in the middle of the night. He'd climbed up on to the ducking stool and he was shouting and singing. Mr

Pleeth told him to get down. Did you really put him in the lock-up, Mr Pleeth?"

"No, missy, I did not. He's not worth the effort of turning the key in the door. You take no notice of him."

John was all ears, sorry to have missed the excitement.

"What was he singing?"

Mr Pleeth snorted:

"Some song by that chap who plays the banjo, what's his name?"

Mrs Pleeth came through from the kitchen and put a fresh pot of tea and a jug of milk on the table. She smiled at her husband:

"You mean George Formby, dear. He plays the ukulele, not the banjo."

"He had a ukulele, did he?" John was beginning to think he'd missed a good show.

"No! No!" Megan burst out laughing. "He was just pretending."

Mummy turned to Mrs Pleeth.

"Who is he? I don't remember him."

"His name is Cyril Roseby. Apparently he was wounded while serving in the army abroad and invalided home. I don't know where he comes from originally, but for some reason he's decided to grace Bartlemere with the pleasure of his company. He's renting a room in Mr Hains' cottage down by the shop. He does nothing but make a nuisance of himself. Causes Walter no end of bother, doesn't he dear?"

Mr Pleeth nodded.

"What does he do?"

"He gets drunk every night and rolls round the village shouting at the top of his voice."

Mrs Pleeth shook her head in disapproval.

"I meant what does he do for a living?"

"He doesn't seem to do anything. I suppose he lives on his army pension. It must be a pretty good one, judging by how much of it he spends on drink."

Mrs Pleeth went back in to the kitchen and returned with a pile of toast. She poured tea for everyone and they turned their attention to breakfast.

"How does Mr Hains get on with his lodger?"

"I don't think he really gets on with anybody. He's a cantankerous old man. He still keeps the old feud going with Mr Martin, after all these years."

"What's that about?"

"Because he reckons Mr Martin tried to steal his girlfriend. But that was thirty years ago. And after all, she married Mr Hains in the end. And she's been dead and gone since before the war. I don't know why he can't let it go."

"Did Mr Martin ever get married?" Megan wanted to know.

"No, he didn't. But that's not the only reason they're still at daggers drawn after all this time," Mrs Pleeth continued. "Mr Martin has carried a life-long grievance towards Mr Hains. Long ago, when he was a young lad, Mr Martin was accused of stealing. His family were tinkers, you know, and people just presumed they would be dishonest. Mr Martin always believed Mr Hains either was the culprit or knew who the culprit was, but he never came forward to clear Mr Martin's name. Mr Martin's never forgiven him for that. You remember that, don't you Walter? Mr Pleeth was at school with both of them, you know."

Mr Pleeth nodded. "About time the pair of them grew up and put it behind them."

"Are there any other newcomers in the village that we don't know?"

"No. Apart from Mr Roseby. And he's one we could have done without." Mrs Pleeth laughed.

"How is Miss Cantrell? Is she keeping well?"

"Yes. Remarkably so, for her age. She's 81 now. Still just the same. She likes her routine. Never changes. Still wearing the same antique clothes." Mrs Pleeth sighed. "I do have a soft spot for her, you know, for all that, she can be – well, let's say – a bit superior. I was in service with her family at Bartlemere Hall, as you know, before I married Walter. She's come down in the world since those days, and no mistake. Never thought I'd see her live like that, all alone, in the Lodge Gate cottage. But she still considers herself a lady of rank, and at her age I don't suppose she'll change now."

"What's happened to The Hall?"

"Nothing. It's still shut up, and dust covers over everything inside. I suppose it'll stay like that until the end of the war."

Megan spoke: "Miss Nicholls is all right, isn't she?"

"She's fine, Megan. You'll see her later at church. In fact, if we're not to be late for morning service, we'd better get a move on."

CHAPTER 7

They were very nearly late for church, and slipped into a pew right at the back. Megan sat between John and her mother.

Megan's eyes were everywhere, looking for people she knew. She soon spotted Miss Nicholls, sitting at the end of a pew near the front. She was talking to Mrs Danson, her mother, who was in her wheelchair in the aisle alongside her.

Megan stretched up in her seat. She could only see the backs of people's heads and the church was crowded. She wanted to find her friends. One by one, she picked them out. Ruth still wore her hair in two neat plaits over her shoulders and Kathleen still had hers in bunches. But Millie had had her hair cut short. As Millie turned towards her mother, Megan could see a pretty slide holding her hair off her face.

Mrs Clarke started up the first notes on the organ. Everyone fell quiet and settled down respectfully. Megan sat back in her place, wishing the service would soon be over.

Reverend Ross came into the church from the vestry, looking calm and dignified in his long robes.

There was always a large turnout at the eleven o'clock service and it seemed today the whole village had crowded into the beautiful little medieval church with its tall tower and glittering stained glass windows.

When the service was over, Reverend Ross stood at the door to shake hands with everyone as they left. Because they were in the back row, Megan and John and their mother were the first to leave.

Reverend Ross greeted them as old friends.

"You must come to The Rectory for tea and biscuits at three o'clock this afternoon."

"Thank you so much," Mother replied, "I'm sure the children would love to come but I have to go back to London today. My train leaves in just over an hour. So this is a flying visit, to bring John and Megan to Mr and Mrs Pleeth's."

"I am so sorry. I wish you could stay."

"So do I, Reverend, believe me! I would love to. But I have to go back to my job in the ammunition factory. It's important war work, so I have a duty to go."

"Of course. I understand. And how is your husband?"

"He's well – so far as I know, the last time I heard. He's been posted overseas with the R.A.F. and letters home don't get through all that frequently. I'm sure you know how it is."

"Indeed, I do, only too well. My son's in the Royal Navy, somewhere on the other side of the world. It's a long wait to hear from him."

Megan went outside into the churchyard, in the sunshine. When she saw Miss Nicholls and her mother come out of church, she hurried up to them.

"Hello, Miss Nicholls! It's really nice to see you again."

"You, too, Megan. I'm so pleased you've come back to us."

"Good morning, Mrs Danson."

"Good morning, Megan. It's lovely to see you. It's been a long while. You've grown up from a little girl to quite the young lady since I last saw you."

Megan smiled. "Thank you."

Megan liked Mrs Danson. She was a nice lady to talk to. She always had time for the children.

Mrs Danson had once been a teacher, too, and Megan was sure her pupils would have liked her as much as Megan and her friends liked her daughter.

It was a shame she couldn't walk. Miss Nicholls had told them her mother had been in a bad accident before the war and ever since then she'd had to use a wheelchair.

It was difficult to push along because of the weight of it. Megan knew that, because when she lived in Bartlemere before, she had offered to push Mrs Danson, but the chair was too heavy for her.

"Would you like me to come and take you out for a walk sometimes? I'm sure now I'm bigger I'll be able to manage your chair."

"That would be lovely. And thank you for offering, my dear."

Megan's school friends came over with their parents. Everyone wanted to talk to her. News had spread round the village that she and John were back.

Megan saw some boys drift over to talk to John. They were all so big, she hardly recognised them. They must be his old friends from the village school. They weren't dressed in short trousers like schoolboys any more. They seemed very grown up. Megan wondered if any of them worked at the farm, too. She hoped so, then John wouldn't be on his own.

Standing in the warm sunshine, among the crowd of friendly faces, Megan couldn't believe it was so long since she had seen them all.

It felt like just last Sunday, not several years ago. It was as if time had stood still in the village. The children had grown, of course, but some things hadn't changed at all. The grown-ups were exactly as she remembered them. It didn't even look as though any of them had had new clothes. Certainly, all the ladies were wearing the same hats.

Mrs Danson had on the same smart maroon jacket she always wore to church, although Megan could remember she used to wear a brooch on the lapel that she didn't have on today. It was a sparkly brooch, in the shape of a bow. Megan had always wondered if they were real diamonds.

She remembered Miss Nicholls' Sunday best outfit too, in navy and white. Megan admired the way she wore her hat, at a jaunty angle. Miss Nicholls was always stylish.

She felt a great rush of affection for the Bartlemere crowd and their warm welcome back.

All too soon, her mother came to her.

"Come along, darling. It's time for me to go. Mr Fairbrother has offered to drive us to the station himself. Kathleen's coming with us, so you'll have company on the way back."

Megan looked over to the pony and trap waiting on the main road. Kathleen was climbing up beside her father on the driver's seat. John was standing beside the pony, talking to Mr Fairbrother.

"I have to go now. Mummy's got to catch her train. I'll see you in school tomorrow."

"Goodbye, Megan. Goodbye, Mrs Michaels. Safe journey."

Megan took her mother's arm and they walked to the trap together.

They made good time to Market Hampton. Mr Fairbrother and Kathleen waited with the vehicle while John and Megan went into the station to see their mother on to the train. It was not so crowded as before and she was able to find a seat.

It was horrible, saying goodbye, standing on tiptoe to blow kisses through the grimy window. The whole train practically disappeared in clouds of smoke and steam as it pulled away, hissing and clanking. The guard blew his whistle and waved his flag. Iron wheels screeched on iron rails. The noise was horrendous.

Megan and John waved and waved as the train slowly moved off beyond the end of the platform. They could see their mother's arm out of the window, waving back. They stood watching until the train was completely out of sight. Even then, they lingered.

The station guard came along, clearing the platform before the next train arrived, shepherding the stragglers back into the booking hall. He was kind but firm. They had to go.

Megan couldn't help crying.

John put his arms round her.

"Don't worry, Meg, I'll look after you. I promise."

Megan hugged him back, wiping her eyes:

"I'll try not to be a misery, I really will."

"Good for you. We're both going to have to put a brave face on it. Now, come on, let's go. We mustn't keep Mr Fairbrother waiting any longer."

John led the way out to the station yard and they got into the trap, Kathleen sitting next to Megan, with John opposite.

When they were clear of the town centre, Mr Fairbrother gee'd the pony up and the trap picked up speed along the quiet country road, their progress marked by the rhythmic clip-clop of the pony's feet.

"Let's play 'I Spy'!" Kathleen suggested.

"All right. You start."

"I spy with my little eye something beginning with P."

"Pony!" John and Megan both shouted together.

"Who said it first?"

"John did, just."

"So it's your go then, John."

John looked all round him for a moment before he decided:

"I spy with my little eye something beginning with H."

"Horse!" Megan shouted.

"Wrong!"

"It can't be horse," Kathleen protested, "we had pony just now. I bet it's hooves."

"Wrong!"

"Hedge!"

"No!"

"Hair?"

"No."

"Hands?"

"No."

The girls' eyes were everywhere, trying to guess. Kathleen tried again.

"Human?"

"That's a good guess, but no. Do you give up?"

"Not yet!" Megan was ready with another guess: "Is it hem, like on my skirt?"

"Wrong!"

"Happy," Kathleen suggested. "I'm happy because you're here."

"You can't see happy, so it doesn't count. Are you ready to give up now?"

Reluctantly, both girls nodded.

"Harness!" John announced, pointing at the pony's back.

"Oh, how stupid of us!" Megan laughed. "So it's your go again."

John glanced round, looking for a hard clue.

"I spy with my little eye something beginning with Y! I bet you can't guess it!"

"I bet we can!"

Despite the sad goodbye at the station, Megan found she was actually enjoying the ride back to Bartlemere, playing the 'I Spy' game with her friend and her brother, as the trap swung gently to the rhythm of the pony's hooves clattering along the road.

Perhaps putting a brave face on it wouldn't be as difficult as she'd thought.

CHAPTER 8

Reverend Ross welcomed Megan and John when they arrived at the Rectory at three o'clock and straight away produced a pot of tea and a plate of home-made biscuits.

"Mrs Judd's speciality. They're very good." He smiled.

Mrs Judd was Reverend Ross's housekeeper.

When they were settled on the big, comfortable settee in the sitting room, Reverend Ross turned to John:

"I know how keen you are on science and how well you were doing in the subject at school. I want to help you keep up your interest."

Megan was delighted. She knew how much it would mean to her brother.

"Thank you very much," John said. "That is really good of you."

"I'm something of an amateur scientist myself, as you know. You shall come and use my microscope and we'll look at slides together and make observations. I have a whole cabinet of slides here. We can prepare our own, too."

"I brought a few things with me," John explained, "like a magnifying glass and a small magnet. I've got a measuring stick and compasses as well."

"Good, good. And you must keep up the habit of recording the results of your experiments in a notebook."

"I've got my notebook," John assured him. "I write in it really small so I won't run out of space. I don't know when I'll be able to get another."

Due to the war, paper was in short supply. At the village school the children had to use slates and chalk. They wrote down their spellings or their sums and when the teacher had called out the answers, they rubbed them out with a rag and wrote down the next thing.

Megan knew that when her brother had attended Bartlemere school before, he had been constantly frustrated that there was no possibility of saving anything he had written.

The reason Megan hated the slates was the chalk dust. It got everywhere. She hated being nearly choked whenever Miss Nicholls said "Now rub your slates clean!"

It would be so different for John, studying here at the Rectory.

Megan had a sudden thought:

"Have you still got Tiger, Reverend Ross?"

She missed the big tabby cat who usually came to check out all the Rectory's visitors.

"Sadly, Megan, no. It's only a couple of months ago that we lost him."

"Did he run away?"

"No. He wasn't lost in that sense. I'm afraid to say he died."

"Oh, dear, What happened?"

"It's quite distressing, really. We think he was poisoned."

"That's horrible. How could he have been?"

34

"I really don't know. I found him outside in the garden, stretched out by the hedge. I'd had people here during the evening, a rehearsal for the play that we're putting on. I don't know if you know about that. Anyway, when everybody had gone I noticed Tiger wasn't about so I went looking for him and I just – well – came across him, lying there."

"I'm so sorry." Megan didn't know what else to say.

"Yes, I was sorry about it, too. He was a character, old Tiger. I was sad to see him go like that. He's buried under the apple tree."

"Why would anyone put down poison?" John wanted to know.

"It was probably intended for rats or mice. Just a shame Tiger picked it up instead of them."

"Who put it there?"

"That's a mystery. Mrs Judd says she didn't, so I really don't know. She was very upset about it. She was extremely fond of Tiger, although he could be a naughty cat at times. In fact, that very day he'd disgraced himself."

"Why? What did he do?"

"Well, Mr Roseby had brought me a rum baba."

"What's that?"

"It's a sort of cream cake flavoured with rum. Mr Roseby said someone had given it to him but he didn't care for them. He liked his beer but he wasn't fond of rum, he said. It certainly did have a strong smell of rum – not the real stuff, I don't suppose, probably rum essence. And a big dollop of mock cream in the middle.

"Anyway, I was expecting these people coming to rehearse the play, so I put the rum baba in the kitchen for later. Naughty old Tiger must have jumped up on the table and knocked it off because when I came through after everyone had gone, I found the rum baba upside down on the floor and the plate smashed. My fault entirely, I should have put it in the cupboard.

"Tiger wasn't allowed up on the dining room table but I never did cure him of jumping up in the kitchen. Well, too late now, sadly."

"Are you going to get another cat?"

"I don't know, Megan. Perhaps. I'll have to see."

Megan thought Reverend Ross sounded very sad. He lived on his own. His wife had died a long time ago. He would surely miss Tiger about the house. She really hoped he would get a new cat soon.

Megan accepted a second cup of tea.

"We saw a poster for your play at the school, Reverend Ross. It's a comedy, isn't it?"

"That's right. It's called 'The Rivals'."

"Are you in it?"

"Yes, I'm playing the part of Jack. Only, he pretends his name is Beverley. That's one of the silly twists in the story. It's all very light-hearted."

"Are you the leading man?"

"As a matter of fact, I am. I'm supposed to be a handsome young fellow. And the joke is that Mr Pleeth is taking the part of my father, and I'm older than he is!"

"You'll have to act really hard at being young, then!"

"I shall, indeed, Megan. And hope the audience uses its imagination! Mr Fairbrother is in it, too. He's playing the part of Sir Lucius O'Trigger."

"That's a funny name."

"It's a very funny role and he's awfully good in it."

"Our mummy said she was in 'The Rivals' when she was at school. She was Lucy, the maid."

"Ah! That's the role Miss Nicholls is playing. And she's having the time of her life with it."

"We heard her rehearsing when we were walking past the school last night, just after we'd arrived."

"Really. We've been rehearsing here at the Rectory. They must have put in an extra rehearsal for some scenes that didn't involve me. I must say, it's taking up a lot of time. We're all working on it every spare minute. It won't be long now before the performance. You are coming to see it, aren't you?

"Of course!"

"And now, John, we must make a regular time for you to come over to the Rectory."

"I start work tomorrow and I don't know what my hours will be yet."

"Well, as soon as you know, you come and tell me and we'll set a date to start."

"All right. And thank you again, very much. I'm really grateful."

"My pleasure, John, my pleasure."

It was time to leave. Reverend Ross saw them out and they walked back together to Mere House.

CHAPTER 9

It was late morning on Monday 26th June. Megan lay on the big bed in the upstairs front room at Mere House. Inside her head, she had just relived the most packed two days of her life. There was so much to think about, so many emotions to deal with.

She rolled over to the edge of the bed and sat up. She felt calmer now. The panicky feeling that hit her when she first saw the body in the water had gone.

It had been helpful to be left alone. She appreciated being allowed to stay in the bedroom by herself all morning. She had been able to let her thoughts fly. Now she felt in control of herself again and able to deal with the normal things of daily life once more.

She got off the bed and glanced round the room.

The most important thing was to let her mother know what had happened.

Her mother had brought a supply of letter-cards from home for the children to use. It took a moment for Megan to remember where she had put them. She looked in the drawer of the bedside cabinet and there they were.

She got one out and unfolded it. Fortunately the glued edges hadn't stuck themselves together, which could happened if the place they were kept in was damp.

Letter-cards were good in one way. They saved paper because you didn't need to use an envelope and they already had a stamp printed on them. But they weren't very big. If Megan and John shared one, they only had a space the size of a postcard each to write on. You had to write really small.

Megan's fountain pen was also in the drawer. It had been her special tenth birthday present. She had remembered to fill it before she left home. Her mother had said a firm 'no' to bringing a bottle of ink in her suitcase, so when her pen ran dry she would have to buy some. There was only one shop in the village so she hoped Mr Porter sold ink.

She knew her mother had left some money with Mrs Pleeth, to be handed out as weekly pocket money. It wouldn't be much, because there wasn't a lot for her to buy in Bartlemere apart from sweets, and they were rationed to three ounces a week. A bottle of ink might need saving up for.

She fished about in the drawer for her precious square of blotting paper. The piece she had was only half the size of a postcard. It was already stained blue with frequent use but she had brought it because she probably wouldn't be able to buy any more.

She thought very carefully about what she wanted to say before she started writing:

Dear Mummy, I love you very much. I wish you didn't have to go home. This morning I saw out of the window that a man had fallen in The Mere. He was dead. It was him who made the noise on Sat. night. He fell off the d. stool. It wasn't very nice & I was scared but now I am OK. There is no school this morning. We had tea with Rev. Ross. Tiger got poisoned. He ate a cream bun and then he died. John has gone to work. I will leave him room to write his bit. Love you loads and loads.

Megan. x x x x

She was pleased with her finished letter. She hadn't done any crossings out so it looked very neat. She left the letter-card open to dry, so she didn't have to use her blotting paper.

Just as she was finishing, there was a tap on the door and Mrs Pleeth put her head round.

"Oh, Megan, you're up and doing. How are you feeling, dear?"

"I'm all right now, Mrs Pleeth, thank you. I was really upset and scared at first but I feel better now."

"Are you sure?"

"Yes. Honestly. I was just writing a letter to mummy telling her what happened. I'll leave it for John to add a bit when he gets home."

"That's a good idea. Now, what I came up to say was this. It's twelve o'clock and you hardly pecked at your breakfast so I wondered if you wanted some lunch before you go to school? There's a new loaf downstairs and some honey from Mrs Willoughby's beehives. Would you like that?"

"Oh, yes please!" Megan suddenly realised how hungry she felt.

By a quarter to one Megan was ready and waiting on The Common opposite the village school. She stood with Kathleen and Millie and Ruth as the other children clustered round. News of the discovery of Mr Roseby's body that morning had flown round the village. All the children seemed to know that Megan was the person who had first seen it, and she was in great demand to tell and retell her story.

In a strange way, going over it again and again helped. She found that each time she repeated what had happened she felt less and less of the original horror that had overwhelmed her when she first saw his body in the water.

Just before one o'clock Miss Nicholls came out of the school carrying the bell. When she saw all the children gathered on The Common she laughed.

"I don't think I'm going to need this, am I?"

They lined up and quickly marched across the gravel path into the one big classroom. It looked bright and inviting on a sunny June day. Megan knew from experience that in wintertime it could be cold and draughty. Today the fire grate was empty and swept clean. In winter a coal fire threw out scarcely enough heat to warm the front row of desks.

Their first lesson was English, which was Megan's favourite. Miss Nicholls read them a paragraph from a book and then picked out some words and asked for their meanings. Megan's hand was the first to shoot up time and again.

Halfway through the afternoon they all went out to play on The Common for a quarter of an hour.

As Megan and the other big girls filed back into school, Mrs Burton, from one of the nearby cottages, was waiting by the door.

Kathleen saw Megan looking puzzled and explained:

"She's come to take the little ones for a nature walk. They go every week."

The bigger boys didn't come back into school either. They were making their way across The Common.

"Where are they going?"

"Monday afternoons they go over to Mr Hain's cottage for woodwork. They use the workshop in his yard. We get needlework."

Back in the classroom, the small group of girls drew their chairs forward in a semicircle round Miss Nicholls' desk. She had cleaned the blackboard and drawn a big, clear diagram on it.

"The girls have each been making an apron this term," Miss Nicholls explained to Megan. "They've very nearly finished, so it's too

41

late for you to make a start now. Daphne Berridge isn't here today so I suggest you carry on working on hers. The diagram on the board shows how to pin and tack the pocket."

"All right, Miss Nicholls."

When Megan unfolded the blue and white gingham and saw how small and tidy Daphne's sewing was, she groaned.

Megan didn't have a lot of patience for needlework. She was always in a hurry to see the finished article and wasn't very bothered about how neat it was. However, she got down to the task and did her best although she didn't think Daphne would be pleased when she saw a big, lumpy pocket on her carefully stitched apron.

When Miss Nicholls dismissed the class she asked Megan to stay behind. Oh dear! Now she was in trouble for messing up Daphne's work. Miss Nicholls was probably going to make her unpick everything she'd done.

She was surprised at what Miss Nicholls said.

"The children are all very pleased to see you again, Megan, but they don't really understand why you've come back. How would you feel about telling the class about your experiences in London and describing what it's like to live there at the moment?"

"What, you mean, get up and speak in front of them all?"

"Yes. You wouldn't be shy about doing that, would you?"

Megan wasn't sure. She wasn't shy by nature, but it was a big thing to stand up in front of everybody.

"What do you want me to say?"

"I would like you to just talk about the danger you faced in London from the bombing so they understand why you've come back here. None of the class has ever experienced an air raid. Your personal story would be very interesting to them."

Megan hesitated. She could certainly tell them about air raids.

42

"Is that all you want me to talk about?"

"Yes."

A moment's more hesitation. Then the decision was made.

"When would you want me to do it, Miss Nicholls?"

"Shall we say Thursday morning, first thing?"

"All right. I'll try."

"Thank you, Megan. That's very helpful."

So it was decided. Now all she had to do was think about what she was going to say.

CHAPTER 10

As soon as Megan got indoors she told Mrs Pleeth about Miss Nicholls' request. Saying out loud to someone else that she was going to give a talk to the class made it seem huge.

"What am I going to say to them?"

"Do just as Miss Nicholls asked you. Tell them your personal story. Describe what you've experienced. I'm sure they'll be very interested."

"But I've got to get up and talk in front of everybody."

"They're your friends. They're not monsters. They won't eat you!"

Megan laughed at Mrs Pleeth's efforts to encourage her. But it made her feel better about it.

She decided to read for a while and went upstairs to fetch her book.

Megan had finished her chapter and was sitting at the dining room table doing a jigsaw puzzle when John came home from work. She called to him as he stood outside the back door kicking his wellingtons off.

"Hello! How did your first day go?"

"Not bad, not bad."

She could see his face had caught the sun. There were grimy streaks on his pink skin. His hair was plastered to his head with sweat. His clothes were muddy and she could see his boots were coated with sludge. But he had a huge grin on his face.

John held out his hands, palms up. Megan got up and went to look.

"John! Look at those blisters! What have you been doing?"

"What haven't I been doing, more like! Digging, heaving bales, carrying buckets, opening and closing gates, leading the horses out to the drinking trough, shovelling muck!"

"That last, I can certainly believe. You pong!"

At that moment, Mrs Pleeth came through to the kitchen.

"Oh, hello John. The worker come home from his day of toil. And I agree with Megan, smelling like it too! Before I let you indoors, young man, you'll need a hose down."

John laughed.

"I'm not joking. It won't be unpleasant on a hot day like this, in fact you'll probably enjoy it. Off you go, into the back yard. And take those wellington boots with you. I'll run upstairs and fetch you a towel and some dry clothes."

Megan burst out laughing. John grinned but didn't argue. He picked up his wellingtons and went round to the back yard where there was a hose attached to a cold tap.

Mrs Pleeth came hurrying back downstairs with her arms full.

"Clear your jigsaw off the table, will you please, Megan, so I can lay the tea. And then go upstairs and wash your hands and tidy yourself up."

As Mrs Pleeth followed John round to the back yard Megan heard her saying: "Where on earth have you been? By the smell of you, you've spent half the day in the pig pen."

Megan broke up her jigsaw, collected the pieces and took them upstairs.

In her bedroom, she poured a little cold water from the big china jug on the washstand into the matching china bowl and splashed her face. Then she scrubbed her hands and dried them. Next, she loosened her long brown hair from its band and brushed it through several times. Finally, she replaced the band so that her hair was off her face. She looked in the mirror on the dressing table and straightened her frock. Mrs Pleeth ought to be satisfied with that.

As she was about to set off back downstairs she heard the door to her brother's room open and shut.

Down in the kitchen Megan helped Mrs Pleeth with the tea. She set the table and made sure everything was ready.

"Go and give Mr Pleeth a knock, please, and tell him five minutes."

Megan went down the hall to the front of the house, to the room underneath her bedroom, and tapped on the door: "Tea in five minutes, Mr Pleeth!" she called. She didn't go in.

She was barely back in the dining room before Mr Pleeth appeared. He must be hungry, she thought to herself. She wouldn't dare say it to him out loud.

A few minutes later John came hurrying down the stairs, looking very pink and scrubbed, his hair washed and combed back. He was wearing clean clothes and didn't smell any more.

"What was that pong? Was it really pigs?"

"Yes!" John laughed. "The other lads found a very impressive way of welcoming me into my new job. They threw my wellingtons in the pig pen!"

"And you went in and fetched them out?" Mr Pleeth enquired.

"Yes – in my socks!"

Mr Pleeth let out a chuckle. "Well then, I guess you passed the test."

"What test?" Megan wanted to know.

"I bet they thought a city boy like John wouldn't want to get his feet dirty. But he proved them wrong, didn't you, lad?"

"Yes, I certainly did."

"Good for you, John. They'll consider you one of the gang now. They won't do anything like that to you again."

"Well, that's a relief!"

"Mr Pleeth, what can I put on these blisters?"

"Let's have a look." John held his hands out.

"Hmm. It'll take a little while for your skin to harden, but give it time and your hands'll be as tough as old leather. Look at mine."

Mrs Pleeth came through at that moment.

"Don't you go telling him to rub anything into his skin, Walter. Those blisters need to heal before anything else. I'll give you some Germolene to rub in tonight before you go to bed, John."

"Thank you, Mrs Pleeth."

"Now, get your tea. I expect you're starving."

None of them needed any second telling. The rabbit casserole disappeared in double quick time.

CHAPTER 11

When the table was cleared and the washing up done, Megan brought her letter-card downstairs and gave it to John.

"I've left you half the space so you can write to mummy, too. But can I squeeze in a little bit more because I want to tell her Miss Nicholls has asked me to give a talk to the class?"

"What about?"

"Air raids."

"That shouldn't be a problem. You know what an air raid is and you never stop talking!"

John dodged out of the way as she tried to hit him.

"Anyway, can I read what you've already put?"

"Course you can."

John read Megan's letter through.

"I'll do mine in pencil," he said, yawning and stretching. "I can't be bothered to go upstairs again to get my pen."

"You'll be able to write more if you do it in pen."

"That's true. All right, then. I'll take it upstairs with me later and do it before I go to bed."

"And you'll leave room for my extra bit?"

"I promise."

Megan spent most of her evening outside, helping Mrs Pleeth water the garden. The big back garden was given over to vegetables. In the front there were some old-established rose bushes. They smelled very sweet in the warm, late evening air.

Megan had come in and gone upstairs to get ready for bed when there was a tap on her door.

"Come in!"

It was John.

"I've finished my letter to mum." He held it out.

Megan laughed as she read his account of the episode with the pigs and his cold shower with the garden hose.

"I've left you a space at the bottom. Then you can seal it down and write the address and post it."

"I'll do that tomorrow."

John sat down on the edge of Megan's bed.

"Meg, why did you put that about Tiger in your letter?"

"What? That he died. Because I thought it was really sad."

"No, I didn't mean that. Why did you put that he ate the cream cake?"

"What do you mean?"

"Well, Meg, you don't know that he did eat the cream cake, do you? Only that he knocked it on the floor."

"But he must have been trying to lick the cream. That would be how he knocked it over."

"How can you be sure, Meg?"

"A cat wouldn't be interested in a cake unless it had cream on. That's what it would go for, surely?"

"So let me get this straight, Meg — you think it was the cream in that cake that poisoned Tiger?"

Megan's train of thought stopped in its tracks. What had seemed so obvious about the cat eating the cream didn't seem so straightforward any more.

"Did I actually say that, John?"

"Look — you've written *'Tiger got poisoned. He ate a cream bun and then he died.'* Reading that, it looks as though you thought the cream bun poisoned him."

"I don't know if I meant that or not, John. That's not what Reverend Ross said, is it?"

"No. He said they had no idea what poisoned Tiger."

"But if he did lick the cream, then it could have been that, couldn't it, John?"

"If the cream was poisoned, yes."

They locked eyes and looked at each other for a long moment. Megan didn't like the way this debate was going and by the expression on his face, neither did John.

"Hang on a minute," Megan said. "Let's think carefully about this. If the cream was poisoned, how did it happen?"

"There are only two possibilities." John was very clear about it. "Either it was accidental or deliberate. Let's start with accidental. How could you accidentally get poison into a cream bun?"

"I suppose if the cream had gone off. It's very warm weather. Perhaps it curdled."

"Cream that had gone bad might make a cat sick, but I doubt it would kill it. And we're not talking about midsummer weather like today. Reverend Ross said this happened a couple of months ago."

"I don't know, then."

"Think about it, Meg. This cream wasn't intended for Tiger. He was trying to steal it. The cream bun was given to Reverend Ross."

Megan reacted with outrage. "You surely can't think someone deliberately put poison in a bun and gave it to Reverend Ross?"

"I think we have to think about it."

Megan did think about it, very hard. She was horrified at the idea.

"Who gave it to him? We'll go and ask them about it."

"He said it was Mr Roseby."

All Megan's indignation disappeared. "We can't ask him about it, can we John, because he's dead."

"Meg, think back. What exactly did Reverend Ross say? Mr Roseby said someone had given the cream bun to him and he gave it to Reverend Ross."

"Because he didn't like the rum flavouring."

"Reverend Ross remarked what a strong smell of rum there was. Perhaps that was to disguise the smell of the poison."

"What poison, John?"

"Reverend Ross thought Tiger had eaten rat poison."

"Wait a minute. If there was rat poison in the bun, covered up with a lot of rum flavour, if Mr Roseby had eaten it, could it have killed him?"

"Probably. Rat poison is lethal to humans too."

"So if he ate some he'd be dead?"

"Yes."

"John – Mr Roseby is dead. Do you realise what this means?"

CHAPTER 12

"Surely Mr Roseby's death was an accident. Oh, please tell me it was, John!"

"If someone had tried to kill him before, possibly it wasn't."

"But why?"

"I have no idea why. But it certainly looks as though somebody wanted him dead."

"That's awful."

"It is, Meg. And even worse, having failed once, I think they tried again."

"Last night?"

"Yes."

"Right outside this window?"

"Exactly."

"I didn't hear him last night. He was climbing up on the ducking stool the night before. I told you all the noise he was making. Mummy and I heard him."

"You said he was drunk."

"Yes. So why didn't he fall in the water then?"

"I'm not sure. But last night he didn't just fall in. The ducking stool went down, and took him under the water with it, Meg."

"But why last night, John?"

"Do you know what kept the ducking stool in place, Meg?"

"I suppose it was fixed down with a weight or something. I don't really know."

"I'm going outside to have a look, Meg."

"What, now?"

"Yes. I'm still dressed. You'd better not come because you're in your night clothes."

"Can I watch you out of the window?"

"Of course."

"What are you looking for?"

"Anything that might give me a clue about how Mr Roseby got in the water."

With that, John was gone. Megan went to the window and settled herself on the wide window sill. It was a clear, bright evening and the sky was still light. John would have no trouble looking around.

Megan began to wonder what was keeping him, when at last she saw him walking up the garden path and out of the gate. He had a brown paper carrier bag with him. He went straight across the road and began scanning the grass around the base of the post on which the see-saw arm of the ducking stool pivoted.

Megan saw him kneel down and take a long wooden box, like a pencil case, out of the bag. He slid back the lid and took something out. Then he stood up. Megan couldn't quite see what he had in his hand, but soon she saw him moving from place to place and setting something down on the grass and making jottings in his notebook. She guessed he was measuring distances.

As she watched him kneel again and bend close to the ground she caught the glint of glass. She thought he must be looking at something through his magnifying glass. Next he seemed to be picking up some small objects and wrapping them up.

He got up and moved around the area close to the post, looking carefully here and there, recording more information in his notebook. Then she watched him straighten up and focus on the end of the ducking stool up above his head. She could see him squinting up into the bright sky as he studied it. Then he turned to look right across the surface of The Mere, as if he was trying to spot something on the opposite side.

He packed everything back into the bag and strolled right round the lower edge of The Mere until he came to a tree practically opposite the ducking stool. He spent a few moments peering down into the water. Evidently he couldn't see what he was looking for because he made no more notes. Then he turned away and walked back to the house.

Megan was waiting for him when he came back up the stairs.

"What did you find? What were you looking for in the water?"

"The main thing I found out was what holds down the ducking stool. I had a vague idea but I couldn't remember exactly what it was."

"Did you find it, then?"

"That's the point, Meg. I found part of it."

"What do you mean?"

"There's a great big iron staple in the ground, like an upside-down U-shape. It must be cemented in because it's rock solid. It doesn't move about at all. You can see there's another similar shaped metal hook on the end of the ducking stool that's now sticking up in the air. What I didn't find is the chain that normally holds the two together."

"So where's that?"

"I assume it's in the water."

"Did it break, then?"

"It might have done, but then again, it might not. I found something that may tell us."

"What?"

"This." John produced a piece of folded greaseproof paper. He unfolded it carefully and it opened up into a flat circular shape. There were several slivers of shiny metal on the surface.

"Mrs Pleeth's been making jam and she had a big pile of these so I asked her if I could have some."

"I know what they are," Megan announced. "You put them on top of the jam before you put the cover on the jar."

"I thought they'd be ideal for collecting specimens to look at under Reverend Ross's microscope."

"Why, what are these metal bits?"

"I'm not sure until I examine them properly, but they could be metal shavings."

"I don't understand what you mean."

"You get shavings when you saw through something, Meg, whether it's wood or metal. It could mean someone sawed through the chain that held the ducking stool in place."

"What, while Mr Roseby was sitting on it?"

"No, I shouldn't think so. But if you knew he was in the habit of climbing up there, you might take an opportunity to saw through the chain when no one was looking, enough to weaken it.

"It might not break the next time he got on the ducking stool, or the time after that, but the chain would be weakened every time. Sooner or later his weight would make it snap and he'd be plunged under the water. If no one was on hand to help him when the ducking stool went down, he probably wouldn't be able to get out on his own.

"If he was drunk when he went into the water, he wouldn't have stood a chance."

Megan and John sat in silence for a moment. They had stunned themselves with the seriousness of the crime they seemed to have uncovered.

"Shouldn't we tell someone?" Megan wondered.

John thought not.

"We don't really have anything to tell yet, except suspicions. I don't think we should tell anybody until we've found out something for certain."

Megan had a sudden thought:

"Did they come and take Mr Roseby's body away? Mrs Pleeth did say everything would be taken care of while I was at school, but I never checked. Only, I would hate to have to go to sleep tonight with him still downstairs in the outhouse."

"Goodness, I hope he's gone." John frowned. "I'll go downstairs and find out."

John was back in next to no time, looking less anxious.

"I asked Mr Pleeth. The doctor came this afternoon and took the body away in a covered cart to Market Hampton. He said it was obviously accidental death by drowning."

"Thanks for that, John."

"Are you all right to go to sleep tonight?"

"Yes, I am now."

"Right. Well, we've done all we can today. Better say goodnight and go to bed."

"I bet you're tired after your day's work, aren't you?"

"I am a bit."

"Don't forget to put that cream on your hands."

"Okay."

"Goodnight, John."

"Night, Meg."

When her brother had gone, Megan got into bed and lay back against the big, soft pillows. With so much to think about, she didn't expect to get to sleep for hours. But despite all the excitement, her eyes soon closed and she drifted off long before Mrs Pleeth crept in to close the blackout blinds.

CHAPTER 13

The next thing Megan was aware of was Mrs Pleeth opening the blackout blinds on Tuesday morning. Sunshine poured into the room.

Megan got up quickly and ran downstairs for her breakfast. She was surprised to see John putting his packed lunch into his bag, ready to leave.

"I have to start work at eight o'clock. I only went at nine yesterday because it was my first day. And they milk the cows at seven, so I'll have to get up even earlier if they teach me how to do that."

"I'm going early myself. I'm walking the long way to school so I can post our letter on the way."

Megan was as good as her word. She left Mere House at half past eight. She turned right and walked down the main road towards the post box, which was set in the wall outside Mr Porter's shop.

Quite a few people were already about in the village. Everyone nodded 'Good morning' as they passed her, and Megan did the same.

As she posted the letter-card to her mother, she heard muttering from the garden next door. She could see Mr Hains stamping about, grumbling.

"Good morning, Mr Hains. How are you today?"

"I'll be all the better if I can get rid of these ants. Little blighters are everywhere. Don't want them in the house."

Megan went to the fence and looked over at the ants. Mr Hains looked up at her.

"I hear it was you spotted my lodger in The Mere."

"Yes, that's right. I'm sorry for what happened to him."

Mr Hains snorted.

"He was nothing but a silly fool, if you ask me. He was asking for trouble, climbing up on the ducking stool. A thing like that's only meant for show. And it's old, been there donkey's years. The man had no sense in his head to think it would take his weight."

"Wasn't he your friend, Mr Hains?"

"No he was not. He was just my lodger, and not a very considerate one at that. And he hadn't paid his rent. I was on the point of asking him to leave, if you want to know the truth."

Mr Hains was scowling. Megan felt as though she had touched on a sore point with him. She quickly changed the subject.

"You were teaching the boys woodwork yesterday afternoon, weren't you?"

"I was, at that. Not that most of them has much idea what they're doing. They're all thumbs."

"I didn't know you were a teacher."

"Well, I'm not, not really. Only Miss Nicholls can't teach them woodwork, can she? Before the war there was that Mr . . . what's his name . . . teaching at the school as well as her, but since he was called up into the army she's had it all to do herself. And I've got this workshop with a big bench and all the tools. That stands here doing nothing, because with my hands I can't do much these days."

Mr Hains held out his hands and Megan could see how crooked his fingers were. They were bent in towards his palms.

"Can't you straighten them?"

"No. That's arthritis, see. That won't get better. I've got no grip and I can't put pressure on a saw or a plane. So I can't do woodwork myself any more. But I can give instructions to the young lads, and provided they behave themselves, I told her I don't mind them coming one afternoon a week."

"What are they making?"

"Teapot stands. Mind you . . ." he laughed, "some of 'em looks more like mystery objects. I've been trying to tell them how to make square corners but they don't all take to my schooling."

Megan thought about Daphne's apron and sympathised.

"I think it's very good of you to do it, Mr Hains."

"Well, I'm a master carpenter, served my full apprenticeship I did, as a lad. Had a lifetime of experience. I figured if anyone should be passing on the skills, it should be me. And I thought if I didn't, they might ask that clown, Martin. Anything would be better than having him do it."

Megan realised she had strayed into dangerous territory again. She didn't want to get drawn into any argument about Mr Martin.

"I've got to go, Mr Hains, or I'll be late."

Besides, Millie was coming up the path towards her, waving. She hurried to meet her and they walked across The Common together to school.

CHAPTER 14

Megan came home from school at four o'clock with one thought in her head.

"Mrs Pleeth, please may I have my ration book. I want to go and get some sweets."

"Yes, of course you can, dear. Have you got some money?"

"Yes, mummy left me sixpence."

"What are you going to buy?"

"I don't know. I'm going to go and see what Mr Porter has got."

"Take care of that ration book. Here, put it in this little bag, with your purse."

"Thank you!"

Megan ran out of the door and made her way along the main road. Mr Porter didn't open until nine o'clock. He closed for an hour at lunch time but stayed open until half past five in the evening, so after school was the best time for Megan to go shopping.

Megan liked Mr Porter. He was a large man. He always wore a brown overall coat which he kept on a peg behind the counter.

The tiny shop seemed too small for Mr Porter with his big, smiling moon-face and the buttons of his overall straining across his chest.

The shop was quite dark inside because the window was covered with notices and posters and piled high with items for sale.

The smell in the shop was what fascinated Megan most. Mr Porter sold everything, so the smell of biscuits and boot polish and bacon and bandages and beetroot mingled into a nameless aroma that tickled her nostrils the moment she stepped inside.

When Megan pushed the door open, the bell fixed above it tinkled loudly.

Mr Porter was already serving a customer. Megan recognised the ankle-length black dress with the high collar and long, puffed sleeves. Even on the warmest day, Miss Cantrell never varied what she wore. Megan smiled at her but said nothing.

Mr Porter's eyes turned to the door and as Megan came in he stopped what he was doing to greet her.

"Well, it's our Megan come back. And look how you've grown! How long has it been, must be two or three years since you were here before. How nice to see you again!"

"Hello, Mr Porter. It's nice to see you again, too. How is Mrs Porter? Is she all right?"

"Ah, she's as well as can be expected. She has her good and bad days. She'll be delighted to know you're here again."

"I'll come and see her soon."

Megan glanced at Miss Cantrell. She always felt uncomfortable around her. She seemed a very forbidding old lady, who expected everyone to stand aside for her and give her right of way in everything.

Megan knew Mrs Pleeth's story that Miss Cantrell had grown up in Bartlemere Hall. She had always been used to a very well-to-do lifestyle with servants waiting on her. Indeed, Mrs Pleeth had lived at

The Hall as a servant before she got married. Times had changed, but Miss Cantrell thought of herself as 'the gentry'. In 1944, most people found that an outdated attitude, but still they showed deference to Miss Cantrell, as much out of habit as anything.

Although she was over eighty, Miss Cantrell still spoke in a strong, commanding voice, as though she never expected anyone to query a word she said.

"Come, come, child. Come here. Mr Porter shall serve you while I make up my mind what I want."

Miss Cantrell stepped back slightly and gestured to Megan to move up to the counter.

Megan murmured "Thank you" as she slipped into the little space Miss Cantrell made.

"What would you like today, my dear?" Mr Porter asked her, beaming.

Megan's eyes ran along the row of big colourful jars of sweets lined up on the shelf behind the counter. Should it be bulls' eyes, or cough candy, or sherbet lemons? Mr Porter waited while she made her choice.

"I'll have an ounce of pear drops, please, Mr Porter."

"Right you are, miss."

Mr Porter kept two sets of scales, his big ones that lived on the floor, which he used for weighing heavy things like potatoes, and a smaller set that he kept on the counter. Megan liked the brass weights that belonged with the small set. They were hourglass shaped and went down in size from one that weighed two pounds and was the size of a tin of fruit, to a tiny little one no bigger than a small button that weighed a quarter of an ounce. They were each fixed to the counter with a piece of string.

Mr Porter picked up the one ounce weight and put it onto one end of the scales. Then he took down the jar of pear drops and unscrewed the lid. Megan watched the sweets pour out into the scoop on the other end of the scales until the two sides were perfectly balanced.

Mr Porter replaced the lid on the jar and put it back on the shelf. Then he picked up a small square of thick, blue paper from the counter, twisted it into a cone shape, and emptied the sweets into it.

"There you are, my dear. Do you have your ration book?"

"Here it is." Megan handed over the ration book and her sixpence. Mr Porter cut out the necessary coupon from the ration book and gave it back to Megan with her change. She carefully put them into her bag, with her sweets.

As Megan turned away from the counter, Miss Cantrell made way for her. To Megan's surprise she spoke to her again:

"How is Mrs Pleeth, child?"

"She's very well, thank you. She's been making jam this week."

"Indeed. She has recovered from the shock of the drowning, then?"

"We were all shocked. It was horrible. But she's all right now."

"Please pass on my regards to her."

"Of course I will. Thank you very much."

"He lived next door to you, I believe?" Miss Cantrell was speaking to Mr Porter.

"He did. But from what Mr Hains says, it wouldn't have been for much longer. It seems he owed him rent and Mr Hains was going to give him notice."

Miss Cantrell shook her head and tutted.

"Not that I was surprised," Mr Porter continued. "He owed me money too. He was always telling me to 'put it on the tab' but he was never keen to settle up. And I hear the situation was the same at The Man in the Moon. He never paid his bar bill."

"It seems to me," said Miss Cantrell severely, "that Mr Roseby was quite an undesirable character."

CHAPTER 15

On Wednesday there was great excitement at school. Edith Williams stepped out to the front.

"I've got an announcement to make. My auntie Eileen, that's my mother's youngest sister, who teaches over in Asherby, is getting married and she's asked me to be a bridesmaid!"

The whole class gathered round her.

"Congratulations!" Miss Nicholls beamed.

"She knows she'll have to give up her job when she gets married," Edith explained, "because you can't be a lady teacher and be married, but it's not that bad because her young man is an American airman and when the war's over she's going to live in America."

The children's excitement overflowed.

"What's his name?"

"What's he look like. Is he good looking?"

"Where in America does he come from?"

"She's going to be a G.I. bride."

"Why do they call American soldiers G.I.'s.?"

"When will the wedding be?"

"What church will it be in?"

"What sort of bridesmaid's dress are you going to wear?"

Edith was overwhelmed by all the interest she had created.

"Hang on a minute! I can't answer all your questions at once! I haven't met him so I don't know what he looks like, but his name's Hank and I think he comes from somewhere in Texas. I don't know anything about my dress yet. The wedding's at the end of August here, in Bartlemere."

"Can we all go?"

"Anyone can go to the church to see them married," Miss Nicholls said. "If there is a reception afterwards, that would be by invitation only."

"Miss Nicholls, you're not going to get married and leave us, are you?" Millie asked.

"No, no fear of that!" Miss Nicholls laughed.

"Where is Texas, Miss Nicholls? Can you show us on the map?"

Miss Nicholls reached up above the blackboard and pulled on a cord. The children stood watching as a big map of the world on a roller gradually unfurled in front of the board. Miss Nicholls took a pointer from her desk.

"There – Texas is on the border of America and Mexico."

"How far is it from here?" Edith asked.

"There's England." Miss Nicholls pointed.

"Gosh, it's a long way!"

"It is, Edith. I don't suppose your auntie will be coming home very often."

"Perhaps you can go and visit her," Ruth suggested. "After all, you're going to be her bridesmaid. I should think she'd want you to go."

Miss Nicholls smiled.

"I think we should save any more discussion of the wedding until playtime. Let's make a start on the morning's work. This is supposed to be an arithmetic lesson, you know!"

She pulled the cord again and the map slowly rewound.

The children went to their seats and got out their slates.

"Today we're going to learn our six times table."

Megan put up her hand: "Miss Nicholls, I already know it, and my seven and eight times."

"I thought that might be the case, Megan. So while we work on the six times, I want you to learn nine times."

"What, all on my own?"

"I'm afraid so, Megan."

"All right." Megan tried not to show how fed up she felt about having to learn a new times table on her own. She nearly had a fit when Miss Nicholls told them they had to know their table from memory by tomorrow.

That evening, as soon as John had come in from work and had this tea, she pounced on him.

"Miss Nicholls says I've got to know my nine times table by tomorrow and I can't do it!"

"It's not that difficult."

"It's all right for you, saying that. You learnt it ages ago."

"Don't worry, I'll help you. You know one nine's nine?"

"Course I do!"

"And what's two nines?"

"Eighteen."

"Three nines?"

"Twenty seven, but I can't remember it after that."

"Go back to two nines is eighteen. What numbers make up eighteen?"

"One and eight."

"And what do those two numbers make if you add them together?"

"Nine, of course."

"Tell me the answer to three nines again."

"Twenty seven."

"And what numbers make up twenty seven."

"Two and seven."

"And what do you get if you add them together?"

"Nine."

"So let's try to work out a pattern for four nines. Look at what you know already. The answer to two times is eighteen, which starts with a one. The answer to three times is twenty seven, which starts with a two. What do you think the answer to the next one might start with?"

Megan hesitated.

"Three?"

"Good guess! And if you're right, what would the next number have to be?"

Megan looked blank. Her brother carried on patiently explaining.

"When the answer was eighteen, you added one and the next number together and they came to nine. When it was twenty seven, you added two and the next number together and they came to nine. So if the same pattern continues, what number would you have to add to three to make nine?"

"Six."

"Of course. You've cracked it, kiddo. Try the next one. What do you suppose five nines starts with?"

Megan suddenly got it.

"Four. And then add five."

"Dead right. Five nines is forty five."

"And six nines is . . . fifty four, and seven is . . . sixty three, and eight is seventy two. Hey – I've really got it."

Megan stared at her brother, who laughed back at her.

"Well done!"

"How did you know that, John?"

"Mr Preston, back in the grammar school, showed us. He was that kind of a teacher. You'll probably get a teacher like Mr Preston when you go up to your next school."

"I won't be going up because there isn't any other school round here, is there? I don't really mind, 'cos I like the village school."

"I know. But you'll move up when we go back to London."

"When do you think we'll be able to go home, John?"

"Don't know. When the war's over, I suppose."

"It's been going on for years and years. Is it ever going to end?"

"It will be over one day. Then we'll go home and Dad will come back and we can all be together again."

"Daddy is coming back, isn't he?"

"Of course he is. Mum always says so, doesn't she? When the war's over."

CHAPTER 16

On Thursday morning, after Miss Nicholls had called the register she turned to Megan.

"Come out to the front," she instructed, "and stand here."

Megan did as she was told, and stood beside Miss Nicholls' desk.

"We're all pleased to see Megan back with us," Miss Nicholls began," but she's not here on holiday. There is a much more serious reason for her stay in Bartlemere. Megan has experienced things in London that are very difficult for us to imagine. She's agreed to talk to us this morning about life where she lives. I hope it will help us all understand more about why she and her brother have had to leave. Are you ready, Megan?"

Megan looked down at her shoes, took a deep breath and nodded.

She could hear Mrs Pleeth's words in her head, 'they're not going to eat you!'

Well, she hoped that was true. Anyway, it was too late to back out now.

Here goes! she thought. She looked up into the faces of her classmates.

"You know my brother and me came to stay in Bartlemere before, for nearly a year. That's when I got to know all of you, because I came to school with you.

"We came out of London then because of what they called the Blitz. There were aeroplanes dropping bombs every night for weeks and weeks. Loads of buildings were knocked down. People said that about a million houses got hit. So loads of families didn't have anywhere to live and ever so many people were killed when their houses fell down. Children got sent away to live somewhere safer and that's when we came to Bartlemere."

Megan paused and looked at the upturned faces watching her. They were all quiet, all listening. So far, so good. She pressed on.

"Then the bombing got less in London. A lot of other places got bombed instead. It was hard luck for them but it was good for us because we were able to go back home."

A hand went up. It was Ruth. Megan stopped. She waited for Miss Nicholls to speak, but she said nothing so Megan looked at Ruth and said "Yes?"

"Did your house get bombed while you were away?"

"No, at least not a direct hit. But the windows got blown out with the blast."

"What about your school?"

"My school was still standing, but my brother's school got knocked down. He had to go to school in a church hall for ages and then they cleared the rubble and they got some like, huts. But a lot of his teachers had joined up anyway, so it was all a real mess for him."

Another hand in the air. Bobby Jackson's this time. Megan's "Yes?" was more confident.

"Did anybody you know get killed by a bomb?"

"I'm not really sure. Sometimes a child didn't come to school any more, and the teacher stopped calling their name on the register. If you knew where they lived, and their house had bomb damage, then you couldn't help wondering what had happened to them. But they might have been evacuated to the country, for safety, like us.

"Anyway, the reason children are being sent away from London now is because of the doodlebugs. I expect you've heard of those?"

Everybody nodded.

"Do they call them buzz bombs?" Jimmy Willoughby wanted to know.

"That's right. And they're called Vee ones, as well. I don't know what that stands for, some German word I think.

"Well, these doodlebugs are different from the bombers that came over before. Like I said, they used to come at night. You'd hear them droning overhead, whole formations of them, making for their target. They used to aim for the London Docks and the factories near the river. They came the same time every night so people would go into their shelter and stay there till the morning.

"But the doodlebugs are different. They come in broad daylight and they just come out of nowhere, really fast. There isn't time for an air raid warning so people can't get into their shelter.

"But the real, big difference is that doodlebugs aren't planes at all. They don't have a pilot in them. The whole thing is a flying bomb. It flies until it runs out of fuel and then it just crashes. When it hits the ground it goes off, and blows up whatever it's landed on."

For a moment there was shocked silence, then all the class began reacting at once:

"That's totally diabolical!"

"It doesn't have a target?"

"It could come down on a hospital!"

"That's terrible!"

"It could hit a school!"

"It drives me mad that anyone would do that!"

"Can't they shoot them down?"

"What do they look like?"

"I've seen one."

Megan's announcement brought quiet again. The class hung on her every word.

"It was on the Sunday morning, a week before I came back here. My brother and me were in the kitchen with our mum, getting ready for Sunday School. We heard this loud buzzing noise. We'd never heard anything like it before. When we looked out of the window we saw this plane, practically overhead. All of a sudden, the buzzing noise stopped and the plane simply dropped out of the sky. The next thing we knew, the whole house shook. And then we could see out of the window a big, black cloud of smoke coming up from where the thing had crashed.

"We forgot all about Sunday School. Our mother grabbed hold of both of us and pushed us into the shelter. We stayed there for the rest of the day. We could hear them keep on coming over. The buzzing was so loud, you could hear it in the shelter. When it stopped, we all held our breath. We knew when it hit the ground 'cos it was like an earthquake."

Millie raised her hand. Megan was fielding questions with ease now.

"What's your shelter like?"

"It's in our dining room. It's a big sheet of iron that rests on iron legs at the corners. And there's like wire mesh in between the legs. It's like a great big iron table, really. Only it's low. You have to get down and crawl into it. We've got sleeping bags and blankets in it. You have to remember, when you wake up, not to jump up quick or you bang your head!"

"Megan?" Miss Nicholls spoke: "When you're in it, how much space is there above your head?"

Megan indicated with her hand. "About this much."

"And three of you can get inside?"

"When my dad used to come home on leave, we all squeezed in."

"All stand up, children," Miss Nicholls ordered them. "Push your desks all together." They jumped to it, pushing and shoving the furniture. There was an earsplitting noise of wood scraping across the floor.

"Now, down you go. Under the desks, everybody."

Megan watched as her friends got down on hands and knees and scrambled under the desks. To her surprise, Miss Nicholls crouched down and got underneath, too.

"Now we can imagine what Megan's shelter must be like," she told the class. "Carry on with your story, Megan. You'll have to sit on the floor as well, if you want us to see you!"

Megan sat down cross-legged at the front of the class.

"Where was I – oh, yes. My brother John said if we counted to thirty after the buzzing stopped, we'd know the buzz bomb had crashed a long way away. So we started doing that. Most of the time, we got to thirty all right. But there was one time we didn't. We hardly got to ten, and then there was this really loud thud and the house shook so much that all the glass broke and fell out of our back windows. It was awful."

"Was it right near you?"

"We didn't know exactly where, but it had to be close. We kept wondering which of our neighbours had taken the hit. It was horrible, thinking about people with bricks coming down on top of their shelter. It must have made such a noise. Or if they hadn't been in the shelter, what had happened to them. We didn't know if it was people we knew. It probably was, but we couldn't go out to see or find out anything.

"My mum had got out and made some tea just a little while before that, but we didn't get out again. We stayed there until the morning.

"Next day, there was glass everywhere, and I mean everywhere. It was a nightmare. It's really difficult to clear up glass because it goes into the curtains and the settee and everything and you daren't sit down in case you sit on a piece of glass. My mum had left the sugar bowl out and we had to throw all the sugar away because you couldn't see the bits of glass in it.

"My mum made her mind up then that we'd have to come back to Bartlemere because it was too dangerous to stay in London. And that's all really. That's my story."

Miss Nicholls got out from under the desk and came to the front of the class.

"I think we should all thank Megan for telling us her story. It's not easy to stand up in front of everybody and speak, and she did it very well. She even answered your questions without getting flustered. So well done, Megan, and thank you."

To Megan's surprise, the rest of the class burst into a round of applause.

Then it was time to move the furniture back into its usual place and carry on with the day's activities. The next lesson was arithmetic. Back to the times tables.

CHAPTER 17

On Saturday morning a letter arrived for Megan and John from their mother.

My two darlings

I was delighted to get your letter. I'm so sorry about the unpleasantness with the man falling in The Mere. What a horrid thing to happen. You were a very brave girl to get up and give a talk in front of the whole class, Megan. Well done! Please tell Mrs Pleeth I haven't found the knitting pattern I mentioned yet but as soon as I do I will send it to her. John, you made me laugh so much with your story about going into the pig pen in your socks. I want to hear all about this job of yours at the farm. Have they let you milk the cows yet? I bet it's all jolly exciting. Rev. Ross is very kind to let you use his microscope. Be sure you thank him each time you go. The Co-Op on the High Street took a hit from a doodlebug yesterday. The shoe repairer's next door was damaged too. You know there's a pillar box on that corner, well that's gone, so I'll have to walk a bit further now to post my letters. But don't worry, I will still write very often, and send you all my love and lots of kisses.

With much love from

Mummy x x x x

After they had both read it several times and showed it to Mr and Mrs Pleeth, Megan carried it away and put it safely in the drawer of her bedside table. She went through the day smiling every time she thought about the letter.

Sunday came round again and John had not yet had time to go for a science lesson with Reverend Ross.

Megan and John attended morning service with Mr & Mrs Pleeth. There were, if anything, even more people in the congregation than last Sunday. The main topic of conversation all week had been Mr Roseby's death and Reverend Ross referred to it during his service.

"We were all shocked and saddened this week at the unexpected death of Cyril Roseby, whom many of you knew. He arrived here in Bartlemere towards the end of last year, when he left the service. I believe he came out of the army on medical grounds, and for reasons of his own he chose our village for his home. Sadly, he was not to be with us for long, carried away at the age of only thirty-three, by a tragic and somewhat unusual accident. Although he would have been the first to agree that sometimes he drank a little more than was good for him, he had proved himself to be a good neighbour to some residents of the village in particular, and he will be sadly missed."

Megan was surprised to hear such a warm tribute. It wasn't the impression she had got of Mr Roseby at all.

Reverend Ross concluded his address with a prayer in the dead man's memory and when they sang a hymn Megan joined in.

On their way out of church Reverend Ross invited Megan and John for tea once again, at three o'clock, suggesting that John stop a little longer so that they could begin their studies.

When it was time to go, Megan went into John's room to see if he was ready. He was just slipping the folded greaseproof paper with the metal shavings into his pocket.

"If Reverend Ross will let me, I'll make a slide out of this and study it under the microscope."

"Will you tell him what you think it is?"

"I don't know. Probably not. It depends how much he asks, really. I don't want to say too much yet."

Reverend Ross was waiting for them with the kettle on and they soon had a cup of tea and another of Mrs Judd's famous biscuits.

"Can I ask you something, Reverend Ross?"

"Yes, of course, Megan. What is it?"

"It's about Mr Roseby."

"Ah, yes. Poor chap."

"How well did you know him?"

"Not all that well, really. Our paths hardly crossed. I know he could make a nuisance of himself when he'd had too much to drink, I'd heard all about that. But what I also know, that perhaps not many other people do, is that he was very kind and attentive to Mrs Danson."

Megan pricked up her ears at that. She liked Mrs Danson and was glad Mr Roseby had been nice to her.

"What did he do for her?"

"He made a point of calling on her several times a week, and for a lady who can't get out of the house unaided, that must have been a great comfort. And he would push her out in her wheelchair, too, some mornings. She had a particular place she liked to sit, looking out over The Mere, not all that far from the ducking stool, as a matter of fact. He used to wheel her out and leave her sitting comfortably there, with her rug tucked round her knees, and then her daughter would take her back home when she came from the school at lunchtime.

"He even used to borrow the pony and trap from The Man in the Moon and take her into Market Hampton once a month for a shopping spree. They'd set off after Miss Nicholls had gone to work, and be back in time for lunch. Half a day, just enough for the old lady.

"Now, I know people had a lot of complaints about Mr Roseby, but I think he showed himself in a different light in the way he looked after Mrs Danson, and I felt I wanted to pay tribute to that in my address this morning."

"Thank you, Reverend Ross. That's really interesting."

When she had finished her tea and biscuits, Megan left her brother and the Reverend setting up the microscope and made her way back to Mere House on her own.

She found Mrs Pleeth sitting outside in the sunshine, knitting.

"What are you making?"

"Socks, for the soldiers. Would you like to come and sit with me and do some knitting?"

"Yes, please. What can I make?"

"Well, squares are always in demand. They make up into such good blankets and have so many uses. I've got plenty of second-hand wool here that I've unpicked from jumpers that people have donated. You choose what colour, and I'll help you cast on."

Megan sat down on the grass and started rummaging through Mrs Pleeth's box of wool. She chose a nice, bright buttercup yellow.

Squares were all plain knitting. She could do one without having to concentrate too hard. It would give her an opportunity to do some serious thinking in her head while her hands were occupied with the wool and needles.

CHAPTER 18

Click-click. Clickety-click. The knitting needles moved but Megan's brain was elsewhere. She couldn't drag her mind away from Mr Roseby.

From what Reverend Ross had said, he sounded like two different men rolled into one.

She could remember his harsh voice singing and shouting on the ducking stool, the night before he died. He'd sounded brash and defiant, and the way he'd spoken to Mr Pleeth was just insulting. No one would have guessed he was a kind man who took an old lady out shopping.

But according to the Reverend, he'd arranged transport to take Mrs Danson to Market Hampton every month. Megan tried to imagine her getting up into the trap. She must have needed a lot of help. And Mr Roseby would have had to lift her heavy wheelchair in and out too.

She wondered what Mrs Danson had bought on these frequent outings to town with Mr Roseby. You could only buy food at the shop where your ration book was registered, and Megan felt sure that would be Mr Porter's shop here in the village. Dress material was in such short supply, due to the war, that there were hardly any clothes to buy. The cottage Mrs Danson and Miss Nicholls lived in was full of beautiful, polished furniture and lovely pictures and ornaments. She wouldn't need to buy anything for the house. So why did she go to Market Hampton so often with Mr Roseby? Did she go to change her library books?

"Megan, you've not got your mind on what you're doing! Look, you've dropped a stitch!"

"Oh! Sorry, Mrs Pleeth."

"I think perhaps you've had enough knitting for today."

Megan agreed. She put the half-finished yellow square aside and stood up.

"I think I'll go for a walk."

"In that case, will you walk over to the Lodge Gate cottage and take Miss Cantrell a pot of jam?"

"All right."

Mrs Pleeth came with Megan into the kitchen and fetched a pot of freshly made jam from the walk-in larder.

"Mind you don't drop it."

"I won't."

"Go straight there and give Miss Cantrell her jam. Then she can have it for her tea. You can take your time on your way back."

"All right, Mrs Pleeth."

Megan wandered off up the garden path and out of the front gate. She crossed the road on to The Common and cut across the grass, making straight for the Lodge Gate cottage.

It was a lovely afternoon and Megan didn't hurry on her errand. Children were laughing and playing in little groups scattered about the big, open space. Whenever she passed near a group, Megan waved, and they waved back.

She dawdled along, enjoying the sunshine, watching the butterflies flitter from one clump of grass to the next.

Eventually, she arrived at Miss Cantrell's house. She walked up the front path and knocked at the door.

After a few moments Miss Cantrell came to the door. She was a tall woman and her long black frock made her look even taller. Megan had to tilt her head back to look up at her.

Miss Cantrell's face was stern and Megan was afraid she was angry at being disturbed on a Sunday afternoon.

She held out the pot of jam.

"Mrs Pleeth asked me to bring this, so you could have it for your tea."

Miss Cantrell's face softened a little. It wouldn't hurt her to smile properly, Megan thought.

"How very kind of her. Please tell her how much I appreciate the thought."

"I'll give her your message."

Megan turned away and the door shut quickly behind her.

Fancy being old and living on your own like that, Megan thought as she walked home. Always dressing in black and being so cross all the time and not even looking pleased when someone gives you a present.

She decided Miss Cantrell probably didn't like children much.

John came back from the Rectory at teatime. Megan couldn't wait for the meal to be finished so she could follow him upstairs to his room.

"Did you put that stuff under the microscope?"

"Yes, we did. And it's definitely what I thought. Reverend Ross says the proper name for metal shavings from something that's been sawn is swarf. And that's what this is. Under the microscope you can see the marks from the saw."

He spread the greaseproof paper disc out on his dressing table and they both stared at the few remaining silvery metal fragments.

"So someone did cut through the chain?"

"It seems like it."

"So they did mean him to fall in the water?"

"Yes."

"What can we do next?"

"Find the chain."

John spread out his notebook and pencil and pair of compasses on the chest of drawers.

"What are you going to do, John?"

"I'm going to try and work out where the chain is."

"How can you do that?"

"Look, the chain must have been under some pressure when it broke, right?"

Megan nodded.

"So it's likely the chain will have been thrown into the air as the ducking stool tipped up. Do you agree?"

"Yes." She could picture in her head the chain flying upwards against the night sky.

"I did some measurements out there the other day. First, I roughly measured the length of the ducking stool itself. I couldn't do it exactly because I couldn't reach but I think I'm about right. Then I measured the distance between the iron staple in the ground that the chain would have gone through, and the post the ducking stool rests on. Are you still with me?"

"Just about." Megan could remember watching her brother through the window as he took the measurements.

"Now I want to try to estimate the trajectory of the chain as it travelled through the air. If I can work that out, then I should be able to calculate where it landed."

"Then we'll know where to start looking for it! That's brilliant!"

"Thank you. But don't get carried away because I haven't worked it out yet," John laughed.

"Is that going to take ages?"

"Probably. I need to get my head round quite a lot of numbers and I'll do it best if I have peace and quiet."

It was Megan's turn to laugh.

"All right. I get the hint. I'll leave you to it. Let me know when you've got the answer."

CHAPTER 19

On Monday Megan started another letter-card to her mother:

Darling Mummy

Thank you for your letter. I'm sorry about the Co-Op. Have there been any more hits on the shops? We went to church yesterday and then John did some experiments with Rev. Ross. I did some knitting with Mrs Pleeth and I took some jam to Miss Cantrell's house. Today Miss Nicholls read us a poem called The Pied Piper about a man who took all the rats away and when they wouldn't pay him he took all the children away. And then we had to draw a picture of him. I don't have any more space.

Lots and lots of love from

Megan x x x x x x

She left room for John to write his letter after hers.

On Tuesday, when John came in from work, he announced that he had just bumped into Mr Martin, who insisted that they call round to see him next day. So on Wednesday, after tea, Megan and John went to visit him.

Mr Martin looked up as he heard the gate.

"Hello, young John. You come to see me at last, and brought your little sister with you?"

"Hello, Mr Martin. Yes, Megan said she wanted to come and see your workshop."

"Did she now? And what might there be in my workshop to interest a young lady?"

Megan didn't answer. She really hoped she wouldn't have to go inside the rickety-looking shed that Mr Martin called his workshop. It looked as though the piles of rusting junk she could see through the door might topple over and come crashing down.

They'd only just got into the yard when Megan nearly fell over a big spade propped up inside the gate.

"You be careful, me darlin'. Don't want you to go hurtin' yourself."

"Have you been gardening, Mr Martin?"

"No, I've not been gardening."

Megan could see earth on the spade.

"Well, digging, then?"

"Oh, aye. Diggin' I have been doing."

He beamed at them and let out one of his hearty laughs.

"What have you been digging?"

"A hole."

"Where?"

"In the churchyard."

"What for?"

"Now, think on it. What do you suppose a hole in a churchyard might be for?"

"I don't know."

Megan had no idea.

She noticed her brother shift his weight on to his other foot. He didn't say anything but he seemed very uncomfortable. Mr Martin was looking at him with a grin on his face.

"He knows, don't you, me lad?"

John didn't answer.

Megan looked back and forth between the two of them, wondering what the secret was.

Still John said nothing.

Mr Martin lowered his voice and said in a mock whisper:

"I've been digging a grave!"

Megan drew back. She had a sudden vision of Tiger, dead by the hedge in the Rectory garden, and Reverend Ross digging a hole to bury him.

"And old Hains supplied the coffin, so for once we was working as a team!" Mr Martin laughed loudly again.

"What does Mr Hains have to do with coffins?" Megan wanted to know.

"Why, he's a master carpenter, ain't he? He makes coffins."

"But he can't work any more because he's got arthritis in his hands."

"Ah, he's got a stock of 'em out the back in his shed. Reckon there's enough piled up in there to serve the whole village!"

"Who was this one for?" John wanted to know.

"Why, Mr Roseby, o'course. It was his funeral today, at eleven o'clock."

Megan and John stared at each other.

"I didn't know that," Megan said. "Did you, John?"

"No."

"Well, seems like a lot of folk didn't know. Leastways, nobody came."

"What, no one at all?" Megan was shocked.

"Nope. The church was empty and only me and the Reverend was at the graveside. And we was both there to do our duty, so to speak. No one else came to see him off."

Megan couldn't believe it. On Sunday mornings the church was always full. To have a funeral service in an empty church seemed dreadful. Even if Mr Roseby didn't have any relatives, didn't he have one single friend who would go? Not even Mrs Danson?

"There's going to be a wedding at the church at the end of August," she told Mr Martin. "I bet the church will be full then."

"Who's getting married? You, young lady?"

Megan burst out laughing.

"No, of course not! Don't be silly! One of the girls at school, Edith Williams, told us she's going to be bridesmaid to her auntie Eileen."

"And who is auntie Eileen getting married to? Some young man from the village?"

"No. He's called Hank. He's an American."

"Is he now?" Mr Martin gave her a long, serious look. "You know about Americans, don't you?"

"No." Megan was alarmed by the tone of this voice. "What about them?"

"Well, to start with, they've got two heads! No, it's perfectly true," Mr Martin insisted, as Megan and John both burst out laughing.

"Whereabouts in America does this Hank comes from?" Mr Martin wanted to know.

"Texas."

"Oh! They've got plenty of money there, from what I've heard. Let's hope Hank owns a big ranch with an oil well on it, then auntie Eileen'll be set up for life."

Mr Martin chuckled.

"Now, you come along o'me and I'll show you my latest gadget, young John."

He led the way through the clutter of his yard and into his workshop.

Megan wondered if he was actually able to do any work there, it was such an untidy jumble. There were bits and pieces covering every surface, littering the floor and hanging down from the rafters.

Megan jumped when Mr Martin pulled out something he wanted to show her brother and disturbed a big spider that scuttled right across the back of his hand.

Mr Martin just brushed it away without a second glance but Megan froze. It was big and black with thick, hairy legs. She began to look around anxiously for any more spiders lurking about.

Something moved very close to her elbow and that did it. Megan decided she would leave John to look at Mr Martin's gadgets on his own.

"I'm going home," she announced, and ran out of the door and back across the yard before they had a chance to reply.

CHAPTER 20

Friday was the last day of term. The morning seemed to drag on endlessly. Miss Nicholls appeared intent on making them work up until the very last moment.

However, in the final half-hour before lunch she brought lessons to a close and told them to empty their desks. Everything had to be taken out.

All their reading books were handed in and stacked neatly on the shelves. Their slates were packed back into the cupboard. Dusters were gathered up and oddments of chalk collected and put into a tin on Miss Nicholls' desk. Bits and pieces of rubbish were thrown away.

As they worked, the usual rule about talking was relaxed and there was a noisy hubbub of holiday excitement in the classroom.

In the afternoon they had races on The Common. All the mothers and grandmothers came to watch and cheer their children on. Megan thought it was very kind of Mrs Pleeth to come and cheer for her.

Megan made a pair with Kathleen in the three-legged race. Trying to run, with your leg tied to somebody else's, made them both scream with laughter. They ran has hard as they could but they fell over three times. Millie and Ruth beat them because they only fell over twice.

All the girls in the class were hopeless at the sack race. Jimmy Willoughby won that, by jumping instead of trying to run.

The boys did much better in the running backwards race, too.

Megan had a chance to win the egg and spoon race but at the very last minute she stumbled and her egg fell on the floor, so Millie beat her.

Mrs Pleeth, who had volunteered to provide the eggs, had very sensibly brought hard-boiled ones, so none were wasted.

By the end of the afternoon, all the children were red in the face and puffed out, but laughing and very happy. They all cheered the winners as loudly as they could. Then Daphne Berridge stepped forward with a bunch of flowers for Miss Nicholls and the grown-ups joined in when the children gave her an extra three cheers.

It was the end of lessons, but not the end of activity in the school. The play was going to be performed the following day.

Instead of going straight home, the children stood outside the school watching, as all kinds of things were brought in.

Megan was surprised to see her brother helping to carry trestle tables and screens and pieces of furniture. At one point John and another lad struggled past her with a huge potted palm.

"That's come from The Rectory!"

"Right." John paused for breath. "Reverend Ross is lending a lot of stuff to put on the stage. We've got to bring it all this afternoon so they can start setting it out for the dress rehearsal later on."

Miss Nicholls came along, carrying a little gilt chair.

"Can we come and see you rehearsing, Miss?"

"No, most definitely not! Besides, you'll be too busy. There's going to be a sing-song outside The Man in the Moon at six o'clock.

Arthur Brown's big brother is home on leave and he can play the mouth organ. Make sure you don't miss it!"

Megan gobbled her tea and was given permission to leave the table early so she could hurry to join her friends outside the pub. Ruth and Kathleen were waiting for her and Millie caught them up a few moments later. The pub forecourt was crowded with people. It seemed practically everyone in the village who was not taking part in the play had come along.

The sing-song got off to a good start. They sang 'It's a long way to Tipperary' and 'Knees up, Mother Brown' and 'Roll out the barrel.'

Claude Brown turned out to be quite a showman. He was a wizard on the mouth organ. When they sang 'Old MacDonald had a farm' he made everybody laugh with all the funny animal noises he put in. To crown it all, he got everybody in a long line and they danced the conga, going into the pub by the front door and out again by the back, and all the way round the outside of the building.

An hour flew by and all too soon it was seven o'clock and time to go home. Before they parted, Kathleen invited Megan and Millie and Ruth up to the farm to play on Monday morning. They agreed to meet at nine o'clock, and Kathleen joked that she would be waiting for them with the bell, to make sure they weren't late.

When Megan came into the dining room in Mere House, Mrs Pleeth was listening to the wireless.

"The sing-song went well, then? I could hear you through the window."

"Oh, yes. It was lovely, thank you. Aren't you going to the rehearsal?"

"No, I'm not," Mrs Pleeth smiled. "My husband has told me in no uncertain terms that I haven't to see him in his costume until he steps onto that stage tomorrow night."

"Do you think he's nervous?"

"Megan, I think he's absolutely terrified!" Mrs Pleeth laughed. "He's never done anything like this in his life before and I don't think he realised what he was letting himself in for."

"Why did he say he'd do it?"

"Reverend Ross can be very persuasive when he puts his mind to it. And they're so short of men. Reverend Ross has even rewritten a couple of servants' parts so they can be played by ladies. In the circumstances I think Walter felt he couldn't refuse."

"Oh, dear. I do hope he doesn't get stage fright tomorrow."

"So do I. He'll never hear the last of it, if he does!"

CHAPTER 21

"The play starts at six o'clock," Mrs Pleeth reminded them next morning, as John was leaving for work. "So we'll only have time for a cup of tea and a biscuit at five. That means you need to tuck in at lunchtime. Dinner will be on the table at one o'clock sharp. You'll be back by then, won't you John?"

"Yes, I only have to work Saturday morning."

"The whole village will be turning out tonight. They're starting the performance at six so it's not too late for the youngsters to attend."

Mrs Pleeth went out into the kitchen to fetch more marmalade.

Megan was glad Mrs Pleeth had mentioned lunch. Thinking about it would help make the time pass. Whenever something exciting was going to happen in the evening, the day always dragged.

Looking at Mr Pleeth's silent, anxious face across the breakfast table, Megan thought he looked as if he would like the day to drag out for ever. He seemed more like a man facing a life or death ordeal than someone who was going to enjoy his new-found fame as an actor.

Mrs Pleeth found plenty to keep Megan occupied during the morning, first peeling potatoes, then cleaning and polishing the silver.

Sharp at one o'clock John, Megan and Mr Pleeth gathered round the dining room table. Mrs Pleeth had made a meat brawn in a deep pudding basin, then turned it out on to a dinner plate. It had set solid in a thick, savoury brown jelly. Mrs Pleeth sliced into the brawn and served a helping on to each plate. There was a bowl of boiled potatoes and another of cabbage to go with it. For afters they had jam tart.

Mrs Pleeth and the children ate up and cleared their plates. Brawn was Mr Pleeth's favourite, but today he didn't seem to have any appetite at all.

After lunch Mrs Pleeth told the children she wanted them to help her in the garden. They spent the afternoon watering and weeding. Megan was delighted when Mrs Pleeth asked her to go into the greenhouse and pick the biggest and ripest tomatoes. This was Megan's favourite task.

"Now you've finished lessons you'll be able to help with fruit picking, Meg," John told her. "They'll pay you, you know."

"Really, how much?"

"That depends. They give you a basket and weigh it when you take it back full."

"Are you allowed to eat any of the fruit, as you go along?"

"Oh, yes. Didn't I say – they weigh you as well, before you start, and again when you finish, so they know how much you've eaten, and then they take that off your wages."

"Don't you believe him, Megan," Mrs Pleeth laughed.

At half past four Mrs Pleeth sent them indoors to get washed and changed, and have a cup of tea and a biscuit before they set off.

"These tickets are not for reserved seats," Mrs Pleeth pointed out. "We need to be early otherwise we shall be in the back row."

She need not have worried.

96

The first few rows were set out with infants' chairs, which were much too small for the adults, so all the children had seats near the front.

"Come and sit by me, John!"

"Meg, I can't get down on to one of those little chairs."

"Of course you can. Come on. Don't go and sit at the back."

Megan had no trouble sitting on a baby's chair. Her brother had to fold himself nearly double to sit beside her, sticking his legs out to the side.

Megan turned and looked around.

Their school room looked so different with the desks removed. Megan wondered where they had been put. Without them, the space seemed enormous.

Chairs had been set out in rows in the half of the room nearest the entrance door. Megan noticed Miss Cantrell in the seat at the end of the row behind her, next to Mrs Pleeth.

The chairs faced a set of makeshift curtains hung from a rope halfway up the walls. In the middle, another rope hung down from a rafter, keeping the curtain rope from sagging. Just not knowing what was on the other side of the curtains was exciting.

The buzz of conversation grew louder as more and more people crowded into the schoolroom.

It was obvious Megan was not the only one who had never been to a play before. It was a new experience for most of the audience, and the younger children in particular were very noisy and restless. Most of them were dying to run and peep through the curtains.

Suddenly, there was a fanfare of music from a gramophone somewhere behind the scenes, the curtains were pulled back and the play began.

Megan sat entranced. She hardly knew or cared what the story was between the characters but she was totally enchanted by what she saw. The costumes were gorgeous, encrusted with gold and jewels. Best of all, everyone had their own hair covered with a big, white wig. They all looked as if they were wearing powder puffs on their heads. They all had a ton of make-up on their faces too, the men as well as the women, with red lips and black beauty spots.

They moved about on the stage in a strange, stiff kind of way, as if they were dancing. They bowed. They curtseyed. Occasionally they touched one another's finger tips.

They didn't speak directly to each other, but mostly faced the front and spoke out over the audience's heads.

Megan didn't even try to follow the dialogue, but those who did obviously found it very funny because the grown-ups laughed a lot.

The big scene between Reverend Ross and Mr Pleeth went off without a hitch and they left the stage to cheers. Megan breathed a sigh of relief.

There was applause every time Miss Nicholls came on to the stage. She looked so pretty as Lucy the maid and she spoke her lines as though her heart was really in them. Megan clapped louder than anyone.

During the break the whole audience went outside on to The Common for a breath of air. As they were filing back into the hall Megan suddenly remembered the night she and her mother and John had walked past the school and heard a rehearsal going on. She couldn't forget how threatening the man's voice had been and how scared Miss Nicholls had sounded.

Megan could remember the exact words the man had said: 'I know all about you and Beverley. Don't think you can keep that a secret from me!'

What had happened to that scene? It had been really tense and quite frightening.

In the first half nobody had said anything like that to Lucy the maid. In the second half, Megan paid particular attention but still she didn't hear those words. By the end, she could only think they had cut that scene out.

Somehow it didn't seem to sit well with the rest of the plot. The character of Lucy was very clever and cheeky and she outwitted everyone she had dealings with.

Megan remembered how realistic the menacing tone of the man's voice had been. Now she had seen the play, it didn't seem to be like anything else in 'The Rivals' at all.

When the curtains finally closed, everyone clapped and cheered. All the characters had to come back on stage again and again to take a bow. It was a very long time before the applause died down and the audience began to file out of the door. Even then, people seemed reluctant to leave. Little groups stood about on The Common chatting and laughing, reliving the excitement of the performance.

At long last Mrs Pleeth decided it was time to go:

"Come along, children. We won't wait for Walter. It'll take him a while to change out of his costume."

Megan called 'goodnight' to her friends and followed Mrs Pleeth and John back to Mere House.

Megan and John had a drink of milk and then went up to bed. Megan undressed and got into bed. She was tired but her brain was far too wide awake for sleep. She could still see the stage in her mind's eye. She slipped a letter-card and her pen out of the drawer beside her bed and started writing a detailed description of the evening to her mother.

CHAPTER 22

On Sunday morning Reverend Ross was all smiles at church, although Megan thought he looked a bit tired. She overheard Mrs Willoughby and Mrs Johnson, in the pew in front of her, talking about a party at The Rectory after the show, so that explained it.

When the service was over, it seemed the members of the cast were having a reunion in the churchyard. They all stood talking together. A cluster of people gathered round them, offering congratulations and telling them how good the show had been. Megan and her friends smiled to see how much the actors seemed to like the attention.

"They're enjoying their fame. They'll all want to be film stars next!" Kathleen joked.

After lunch Megan went back to composing her letter to her mother. Although she thought carefully about every word before she wrote it, and squeezed her writing as small as she could, there still wasn't enough space on half a letter-card to answer her mother's latest letter and cram in everything she wanted to say about the play.

She wanted to finish it so John could write his half tonight. Then she would post it tomorrow.

That meant, all being well, her mother would get it by the weekend.

The post was collected once a day in Bartlemere by horse-and-cart and taken to Market Hampton. In the town, post was carried on short runs by motor, but petrol was strictly rationed so horse-drawn vans were used too.

Delays happened all the time. The war had disrupted the post everywhere. No end of postmen had left their jobs to join up, and in many places women had taken over their work. They put in long hours in sorting offices, walked the delivery rounds in all weathers carrying heavy sacks and even drove the mail vans.

Of course, bombs were not choosy where they fell. Long-distance mail went by train and if the line was out of action due to an air raid, it didn't get through.

A letter box or post office could take a hit, and then all the letters and parcels inside were lost.

When you put a letter in the post you just had to cross your fingers and hope for the best.

At teatime, Megan helped Mrs Pleeth lay the table. Mr Pleeth came and sat down, looking much more relaxed than yesterday.

"I though you were brilliant, Mr Pleeth," Megan told him.

"Thank you, my dear."

"Did you enjoy doing it?"

"In some ways, yes. Although I have to admit, I found it rather nerve-racking."

"But you're not sorry you did it, are you?"

"You're not, are you Walter?" Mrs Pleeth prompted, coming through from the kitchen with a glass dish of homemade piccalilli.

Mr Pleeth smiled:

"No. I'm not sorry."

"So you'd do it again?"

"Now, wait a minute, I never said that!"

Everybody burst out laughing.

By mid-evening the weather had turned overcast and it felt muggy, as if a storm was brewing.

Megan couldn't settle to anything. She picked up her knitting bag and got out her yellow square, but then remembered she had dropped a stitch. She couldn't be bothered to unpick what she had done to find the mistake and put it right. The knitting went back in its bag.

She tried to settle down with a book. First she picked up a collection of poems, then a picture book about the Egyptian pyramids, but neither could hold her attention. Finally, she threw them both aside and settled for Enid Blyton's 'Five on a Treasure Island'. She'd already read it several times before and could thumb through the pages without having to give it much concentration.

What was niggling her was that missing scene from the play. For some reason she couldn't explain, she couldn't get it out of her mind.

The storm broke in the night while Megan was fast asleep and she slept through it. By morning, the sun was out again and the air was fresh and clear. Megan jumped out of bed at her usual time and went through her regular getting-up routine, to be sure she would be at Kathleen's by nine o'clock sharp.

She met Millie and Ruth at the farm gate and they went up the long, rutted track together. Kathleen was waiting for them at the farmhouse door, waving as they walked towards her.

They had the whole morning ahead of them and they each took a turn to choose what game to play. The time flew by, and when Mrs Fairbrother told them they were invited to stay for lunch, they were happy to sit in the big farmhouse kitchen and have sandwiches and milk.

After that they wandered outdoors and back inside again; they followed Mr Fairbrother when he went to harness up the pony and trap; they went to look at the cows; and then they had their favourite dolls' tea party again.

Megan couldn't believe they had been allowed to stay at the farm all day. She was even more surprised when Kathleen's mother said that they were all staying for tea.

"And your brother John is having tea with us, too," Mrs Fairbrother told her.

"What are we having?" Kathleen wanted to know.

"Sausage and mash, and you girls can help me peel the potatoes."

It was a lively, happy gathering round the tea table, and Mrs Fairbrother had no shortage of helpers with the clearing away and washing up.

John seemed to Megan a bit quiet and rather uncomfortable. Megan thought that must be because he was with so many children younger than himself, and all girls too. But John was never as noisy as she was, anyway.

It was practically bedtime when they gathered up their belongings to leave. Megan and John were ready to go when Millie's mother appeared at the door, and just behind her was Ruth's mother. The girls hadn't expected to be fetched so it was a surprise to see their mothers. They all said a tired 'goodnight' and set off home.

Megan picked up John's quiet mood and didn't attempt to make conversation with him on their way to Mere House. He led the way round to the back door and they came into the kitchen and through into the dining room.

Megan put her bag down and turned to Mrs Pleeth, who was sitting at her usual place at the table, an untouched cup of tea in front of her. Immediately, Megan could see something was very wrong.

"What is it, Mrs Pleeth? What's happened?"

"Oh, Megan, I'm afraid there's been an accident. A terrible accident."

CHAPTER 23

Megan looked from Mrs Pleeth to her brother and back again, in amazement.

"What's happened? Who . . .?"

Mrs Pleeth seemed unable to get out any more words. John quietly took up the story.

"There's been an explosion at Mr Hains' cottage, Meg."

"An explosion? What, like a bomb?"

"Sort of. A small one."

"What do you mean?"

"Well, it wasn't a bomb dropped by a plane. But it did explode."

"What about Mr Hains, is he all right?"

"No, Meg."

"Is he hurt? What's happened to him?"

John looked at her but didn't answer. Megan's brain started buzzing as if it was on fire.

"John?"

"He's dead, Meg."

"Mr Hains? He can't be!"

"I'm sorry, Meg. But he is."

"When did it happen?"

"About eleven o'clock this morning. Mr Pleeth told us not to tell any of you younger ones until everything had been . . . tidied up . . . at his cottage. That's why you were kept at the farm all day."

"So Mrs Fairbrother knew?"

"Yes. And Mr Fairbrother. He took Mr Pleeth to Market Hampton this afternoon. They're not back yet."

Megan remembered watching Mr Fairbrother getting the pony and trap ready for the road. She had never guessed anything was wrong. Mr Fairbrother's acting had been every bit as good then as it had been on the stage on Saturday night.

"And Millie and Ruth?"

"Their mums knew. That's why they came to take them home, so they could tell them."

Megan flopped down on the chair opposite Mrs Pleeth, trying to keep her flying thoughts under control.

"What happened?"

Before John could answer, Mrs Pleeth spoke:

"Mr Pleeth thinks Mr Hains received a package in the post. He was sitting outside his door, as usual. When he undid the parcel it blew up. It knocked him back off his chair and he hit is head against the wall as he fell. He didn't get up again."

"How awful."

"It's a blessing he was outside. If it had gone off indoors, Walter says it could have set fire to the cottage and burned it to the ground. There was a bit of a breeze today. Who's to say a fire wouldn't have spread and taken two or three other cottages with it."

There was silence in the dining room. Megan heard the ticking of the clock on the wall as loud as drum beats.

106

"Would you like me to make you a fresh cup of tea, Mrs Pleeth?" John asked.

"What dear? Oh, yes, please. That would be much appreciated."

"Meg?"

"Please, John. I'll help you."

They both went out into the kitchen. John filled the big black kettle and set it on the stove. Megan went to the cupboard to get out cups and saucers. They passed in the middle of the kitchen. John held out his arms and Megan fell against him, hot tears scalding her face. He held her close as the shock burst out of her in big, shuddering sobs.

By the time the kettle boiled, Megan had calmed down a bit, although when she put the teaspoons out they rattled in the saucers.

They sat round the table together over their tea, silent because no one knew what to say. To see Mrs Pleeth tense and lost for words was unknown. Megan felt she wanted to do something to help her but she didn't know what she could do.

It was John who got up from the table a little while later and said:

"Come along, Meg. It's time you went to bed. Look, if you can't sleep or you're worried in the night, just come and knock on my door."

"Thank you." Megan gave him a hug and he hugged and kissed her in return.

"Goodnight, Mrs Pleeth. I hope Mr Pleeth will be back soon."

"Goodnight, dear."

As Megan left the room, John switched on the table lamp and started clearing away the tea cups.

Megan went upstairs. As soon as she was in her room she closed the faded pink curtains, went through her regular bedtime routine of face-washing and teeth-cleaning, using the big china bowl on the washstand.

She changed into her nightdress and lay down on the bed.

Another death in the village, so soon. It was only two weeks since Mr Roseby's drowning. Only five days since his burial.

She remembered the conversation she and John had had with Mr Martin after the funeral. How shocked she had been that nobody had gone.

It would be different with Mr Hains, she felt sure. He had lived his whole life in Bartlemere and the village was full of people who had known him all those years. Even if he hadn't been particularly popular, people didn't like to speak ill of the dead. They would remember his good points, what a skilled craftsman he had been, his wife who had died before the war.

At least now the stupid feud between Mr Hains and Mr Martin was over, Megan thought.

In her head, she could hear Mr Martin's cheery voice: 'Old Hains supplied the coffin, so for once we was working as a team!'

Would Mr Hains be buried in one of his own coffins? What a macabre idea.

Would Mr Martin dig his grave?

Would that burial count as teamwork, too, Megan wondered, if one of the team was dead?

Much later, in the early hours of the morning, Megan was awoken by the sound of voices and horse's hooves under her window. She got out of bed and went to peep out. To her surprise, the blackout blinds had not been drawn. Megan hastily pulled them shut. Mrs Pleeth had forgotten to do it. She had never forgotten before. Megan realised how preoccupied she must be.

Megan was in time to see the back of the trap disappearing into the darkness, and she heard the front door close.

She slipped back into bed. Mr Pleeth and Mr Fairbrother had been gone hours. They must have been at Market Hampton police station all this time, talking about what had happened to Mr Hains.

Megan couldn't believe he had been killed by a bomb. She and John had left their mother and home behind, and come all the way to Bartlemere just to get away from bombs. And now here was one exploding in the middle of the village. If that was going to happen here, they might as well go home.

But the bombs in London were different. They fell anywhere, could kill anyone. This little bomb, which had been delivered by the postman to Mr Hains, could only have been meant for him.

The postman! They must have been questioning him at the police station to find out if he knew what was in the parcel he delivered.

Megan tried to remember what the postman looked like but she couldn't. He usually came when she was at school so she didn't see him.

But who in the world would send Mr Hains a bomb in a parcel? When it exploded it could have blown his fingers off, or gone in his eyes and blinded him. Even if they didn't intend him to die, whoever sent it must have really wanted to hurt him.

Who on earth hated Mr Hains so much they would do that to him?

A horrible cold, creeping dread came over Megan as one name, and one name only, sprang into her mind.

CHAPTER 24

It was true, Mr Martin and Mr Hains had never got on, but surely Mr Martin wouldn't try to kill him. Never in a million years.

The last time she had talked to Mr Martin, he had been laughing about him and Mr Hains working as a team, really laughing about it. He didn't hate Mr Hains so much that he'd set out to harm him. Did he?

Mr Fairbrother hadn't shown a trace of what must have been going through his mind when he got the pony and trap ready yesterday, with Megan and the others watching. He had spoken to them quite normally. Even Kathleen, his own daughter, had not guessed anything was wrong.

Grown-ups could be good actors. All the people they had watched on Saturday night proved that. They'd watched people they all knew well, pretending to be something they weren't, and everybody believed in them.

Everybody knew about the feud between Mr Hains and Mr Martin. Even if she believed Mr Martin would never do such a terrible thing, suppose the police thought he might! Would they arrest him?

Megan decided there and then that first thing in the morning she would go and visit Mr Martin to make sure he was all right and tell him she believed he was innocent.

It was hard to go back to sleep. Eventually she gave up trying. She switched on her bedside lamp and got her writing things out of the drawer.

She felt a bit better when she had spilled out her anxieties in a letter to her mother. She put the light out and tried to settle down. But still she tossed and turned and hardly closed her eyes again before morning.

As soon as she heard her brother getting up, she got up too. She followed him down for his breakfast. Mrs Pleeth made no comment about Megan's early start to the day. She looked as if she had been up half the night herself.

As Mrs Pleeth busied herself in the kitchen, Megan spoke urgently to John.

"I'm really worried about Mr Martin. I want to go and see him. I think we should go on your way to work. I'm going anyway, but I would really like it if you came with me."

"All right, Meg. I've been thinking about him, too. It's a good idea of yours. We'll walk past his place and check that he's all right."

"Hurry up, then."

They were out of the door in no time and walked straight up the path opposite Mere House. At the church, they took the path running off to the left, past Miss Nicholls' and Mrs Danson's cottage.

The rickety gate to Mr Martin's yard was shut and so was the workshop door, beyond. The front of the cottage itself was quiet, all the windows closed but the curtains open.

The let themselves in through the gate in the yard and went round to the back door.

It was shut. Megan knocked. No answer. She glanced round at John, who was at her shoulder.

"Should I try the door?"

"Yes."

She put her hand on the door knob and turned it. The knob moved slightly under her fingers but the door stayed firmly shut.

"It's locked."

John stepped over to the kitchen window and peered in.

"He's not here."

"John, you don't suppose they've taken him away, do you?"

"I don't know what to think, Meg. It's a possibility. Look, I've got to go. I mustn't be late for work. You do whatever you can to find out what's happened to Mr Martin."

"Who should I ask?"

"Well, if he is in police custody, the person who can tell you is Mr Pleeth."

Megan ran back to Mere House as fast as her legs would carry her. She burst in through the kitchen door and stopped when she saw Mr Pleeth sitting over his breakfast in the dining room.

"Mr Pleeth, what's happened to Mr Martin?"

Mr Pleeth looked up but didn't answer right away. He was wearing his police constable face, the look he always had when he was on official police business. It made Megan feel uneasy.

She thought he was going to grumble at her because she had forgotten to say 'good morning'. She didn't care. She pushed on.

"He's not at home. Do you know where he's gone?"

"I'm sorry to have to tell you," Mr Pleeth replied heavily, "that since yesterday teatime, Mr Martin has been held in a cell at Market Hampton police station."

"Why? What's he done? They don't think he had anything to do with Mr Hains getting bombed, do they?"

Mrs Pleeth came in from the kitchen and stood beside Megan.

"Mr Martin is helping the police with their enquiries," Mr Pleeth explained.

"He's been arrested?"

"No. He agreed to go with them voluntarily to answer some questions."

"When's he coming back?"

"If he's able to give a satisfactory account of himself, he'll be allowed to come home today or tomorrow. If not, well, they'll keep him there a bit longer."

"What will they do to him?"

"That depends." Mr Pleeth cleared his throat and shook his head once or twice. Megan thought he looked like a dog trying to get water out of its ears. He seemed reluctant to answer to her.

"What does it depend on? Please tell me what's going on, Mr Pleeth."

"The police have to look hard at anyone who was known to have a grudge against Mr Hains. It's only natural they should want to talk to Mr Martin. It's well know there's been bad blood between the two of them for years. None of us would like to think it might have come to this, but we have to face it, Megan. Someone who didn't like Mr Hains sent him that parcel. He hardly knows anybody outside the village, so it's going to be someone we all know. I don't like that thought any more than you do, let me tell you. Anyways, you might as well know they're talking about searching his workshop. He's got that much stuff in there, I'd be surprised if they didn't find something you could make an explosive with."

Mr Pleeth shook his head again, as though he would like to dislodge the thought if he could.

Mrs Pleeth went out into the kitchen again and Megan could hear her putting the kettle on.

"If they do find something, and they really think he did it, what will happen then?"

"They'll charge him with murder, like as not. Or, I suppose it could be manslaughter."

"What's that?"

"That's causing a death when you didn't actually mean to, but the person ended up dead anyway. Like if he was to say he sent it to him to scare him, but he didn't have any intention of killing him."

"You couldn't send somebody a bomb and not think it might kill them."

"Precisely. I don't think he's likely to get away with manslaughter."

"So would he have to go in front of a judge?"

"He would, a judge and jury. Twelve good men, and true. They'd listen to all the evidence and then they'd give their verdict. Guilty or not guilty."

"What would happen to him if he's found guilty?"

"He'd be hanged. That's the penalty for murder in this country. Why, that chap Kemp was executed at Wandsworth prison in London only a month ago."

"And if he's not guilty?"

"Then they'll let him go free."

"So that's it? Either he's put to death or he goes home. Isn't there anything in between?"

"No. Not unless he pleads insanity, of course. That's always a possibility under the McNaughton rules."

114

"What's that?"

"They're the rules judges use to decide whether a person is insane or not." Mr Pleeth cleared his throat again and quoted in his very official police voice: "If he was labouring under such a deficit of reason from disease of the mind to not know the nature and quality of the act; or that if he did know it, that he did not know that what he was doing was wrong."

"Mr Martin's not insane."

"No, I don't think he is. But it's something the lawyers like to try on."

"What would happen to him if they thought he was insane?"

"Then they'd lock him up for the rest of his life."

"Oh, I can't bear this. It's horrible! Horrible! Mr Martin hasn't done anything, I'm sure of it. I don't want to think about any of this!"

Megan turned and fled out of the dining room, choking back tears. She ran upstairs to her room and flung herself on the bed.

Of course Mr Martin wasn't a murderer. Of course he wasn't insane. Only, some judge might think that if he wasn't the one, then he must be the other.

What a nightmare for Mr Martin. What a nightmare for them all.

CHAPTER 25

Mrs Pleeth decided that activity was the best way to deal with the stress and uncertainty that had descended on the household. All that day, and the next, she conducted a campaign of spring-cleaning from top to bottom of Mere House.

And all the while, she never let Megan out of her sight. When they were not pegging out things to dry on the washing line, they were rehanging curtains and emptying cupboards.

Mr Pleeth, meanwhile, shut himself away in his office with his incident book and a big pile of official-looking reports, or went tramping round the village on his duties.

On Wednesday evening John came in from work and announced before he was barely inside the back door:

"He's back!"

Megan did a dance of delight round the kitchen.

"Where's Mr Pleeth, Meg?"

"He's out."

"Mrs Pleeth?"

"She's putting away ironing in the airing cupboard."

"Go and shout her."

Mrs Pleeth came hurrying into the dining room.

"What's the news, John?"

"I came past Mr Martin's place on my way home from work, and he was in the yard. He said they'd brought him back a couple of hours ago. They say they may want to speak to him again but they haven't charged him with anything. They've had a good poke around his workshop but found nothing suspicious. So it looks like he's in the clear."

"Thank goodness! Oh, I wonder if Walter knows."

"Hooray! Hooray!" Megan was doing a war dance round the dining table.

"Mr Pleeth was there, actually. I think he may have been one of the people who searched the workshop."

"He's been out all day," Mrs Pleeth sighed, "but of course I never know what police business he's on. Oh, it is difficult, when it's someone you've known all your life. They were at school together as boys, all three of them. I wonder if he'll be late for his tea."

"I don't think so. It looked as if the other men were getting ready to go. There's a big black car parked outside The Man in the Moon. I presume that's the police car. I don't think they'll be long."

"A police car! Can I go and have a look?"

"No, Megan!" Mrs Pleeth put her foot down. "No running out to stare! It's bad manners."

"But you can't see the front of the pub without going outside."

"Then you'll have to do without seeing it. You've seen it before plenty of times."

"But the police car . . ."

"I said no, Megan."

Megan gave up. Mrs Pleeth brought a pile of plates to the dining room doorway and Megan took them from her and began to lay the table.

"Can we go and call on Mr Martin after tea?"

"If Mr Pleeth says it's all right, you may go."

"What's for tea tonight?" John was trying to change the subject, calm tempers.

"Woolton pie."

Megan screwed up her nose. Boiled root vegetables with a pastry topping was not her favourite meal. They had it all too often in London because there was so little meat in the shops and when it was available the weekly ration was so small.

John frowned at her: "Don't be difficult, Meg. I'm hungry. I'll eat anything."

"We can go and see Mr Martin directly after tea, can't we?"

"If Mr Pleeth says it's all right."

Mr Pleeth arrived a few minutes later. He quickly washed his hands and was sitting at the table with the children when the pie came out of the oven. As soon as he came in the back door Mrs Pleeth started to look more relaxed. She served them all and began passing round the gravy.

"John says Mr Martin's back home, Walter."

"Yes, I'm pleased to say."

"We can go and see him, can't we, Mr Pleeth?" Megan pleaded.

"Yes. Provided he's willing to have visitors."

"Oh, good!"

Megan's pie tasted all the better for knowing that.

She ate her stewed fruit and custard as quickly as she could and when they had all finished she was first down from the table.

As she and John walked up to Mr Martin's cottage they could see him through the window of his workshop. He heard the gate and turned as they came into the yard. He beckoned to them.

"Come in, come in, me darlin's. Good to see you. Very nice of you to come and pay me a visit."

"Are you all right, Mr Martin?"

Megan stared up into his face, anxious to see that he looked the same as usual.

"I'm quite well. In fact, I'm doing fine. Do you know what, I've had a little holiday in Market Hampton. I was given board and lodging, and they brought me home, practically to me door. I got a ride in a motor car, think on that! And to top it all, some kind gentlemen have been and tidied up me workshop for me! So I've had a good couple of days, thank you very much, me darlin'!"

He beamed at them, his dark eyes crinkled up at the corners in a big smile.

"But are you really all right? Weren't you scared? " Megan knew he was making a joke out of his experience with the police.

Mr Martin let the smile fade and looked at them both seriously.

"Yes, I was. I'll admit that to you. It shook me up a bit when I heard what had happened to old Hains, and it shook me up a good deal more when I realised some people thought I might have had a hand in it. I'm very lucky the police listened to what I said and believed I was telling the truth, and they've let me come home. And it means a lot to me that I have friends in this village who'd take my part and stick up for me, and I know the two of you are two of them friends, and I'm very grateful."

He held out his hand to each of them in turn. First John and then Megan shook hands with him. It was a solemn moment.

Then he grinned at them again: "Now let's have a look and see how many spiders those fellows disturbed when they was turning my workshop upside down!"

CHAPTER 26

As they rooted around in Mr Martin's workshop, Megan kept a sharp eye out for spiders.

Mr Martin picked up a small pear-shaped piece of metal attached to a piece of string.

"There you are, John me lad. You can have that, if you'd like."

"Thank you very much, Mr Martin."

"What is it?" Megan wanted to know.

"It's a plumb line. You hold it up like this," Mr Martin demonstrated, "and the string hangs down in a straight line because of the weight on the bottom. So if you hold it by a wall and mark top and bottom, you can be sure you'll have a straight line between."

John pocketed his present.

"Now, let's see if we can find anything for you, me darlin'." Mr Martin carried on picking through various things on the workbench and looking in boxes to see if he could find something to give to Megan. She didn't think he'd find anything she would want to take home, but when he turned up a small carton of coloured chalks, she accepted the gift with pleasure.

They went home not long after, glad to leave Mr Martin in good spirits and not too upset by his experiences of the past couple of days.

"I'm really glad they let Mr Martin go," John said, as they walked back past The Mere and the ducking stool, "but the question is, if he didn't send Mr Hains that parcel, then who did?"

"How can you make a parcel blow up?"

"That's a good question, Meg. Obviously, you'd need some kind of explosive."

"What, like dynamite?"

"Yes, but an ordinary person can't just go out and buy dynamite. You'd have to use something easy to get hold of. I've heard of bombs being made out of weed-killer, but I've no idea how you'd make one."

"Weed-killer? Isn't that poisonous?"

"Yes, I think so."

"You'd have to be jolly careful then, that while you were making your bomb you didn't poison yourself."

"You'd have to be careful not to set the bomb off while you were making it, or you'd blow yourself up."

"What kind of person would make something like that, John?"

"Some kind of lunatic, I'd say."

As they let themselves in through the back door, Mrs Pleeth emerged from the walk-in larder.

"How is Mr Martin?" She couldn't keep the anxiety out of her voice.

"He's all right. At first, he made a joke of it," Megan explained, "and tried to pretend it was nothing. But then he did admit it had upset him. But in the end the police believed him, that he didn't have anything to do with it."

"The police kept him at Market Hampton for two days, didn't they?" John said. "If he had any guilty secret, I'm sure they would have found it out in that time."

"And they didn't find anything bad in his workshop," Megan added.

"I'm glad to hear it's ended well for him." Mrs Pleeth looked relieved at their news. "This has been such a shocking thing."

Suddenly she noticed the clock.

"Goodness me, look at the time! It's time you both went up to bed."

They said their goodnights and went upstairs.

The following morning it was obvious Mrs Pleeth intended to keep Megan in her sights again. After the breakfast things were cleared away and washed up, she went into the larder and fetched out a dish covered in greaseproof paper. She carefully put it into a brown paper carrier bag.

"Last night I made a separate, small Woolton pie for Miss Cantrell. We'll walk over together and take it to her."

Their route took them past Mr Hains' cottage and as they approached the fence, Megan was glad Mrs Pleeth was with her.

In London, Megan had seen houses that had been bombed in night-time raids. Walking to school the next day, it was horrible to see roof and walls blown away, window glass gone, people's bedroom wallpaper on public display. She dreaded what sight would meet her eyes at Mr Hains' cottage.

They slowed as they reached the gate. To Megan's surprise, there was nothing out of the ordinary to see. She had expected there to be damage, or blood dripping down the brickwork. But there was nothing to point out where Mr Hains had fallen. The path had been swept and everything looked neat and tidy in the morning sunshine.

The only sign that anything had happened was in the flowers border where plants lay crushed and broken. Megan guessed they had been trampled on when people who heard the explosion came running to help.

"What will happen to the cottage, Mrs Pleeth?"

"I really don't know, dear."

"Did Mr Hains have any relatives?"

"He has one daughter, Mary. She's serving in the Wrens, somewhere in Wales or Scotland. She's being contacted. Mr Pleeth has put that in hand."

Standing there at the gate with everything looking so normal, Megan found it difficult to believe that Mr Hains wouldn't come stamping out of his door at any minute, frowning at them from under his brows, as he always did, telling them what was wrong with the day.

She turned away, and walked beside Mrs Pleeth along the gravel path until they turned aside, opposite Millie's house, and crossed over the corner of The Common to the Lodge Gate cottage.

Mrs Pleeth knocked, and moments later the familiar tall, black-clad figure opened the door.

CHAPTER 27

Megan had never been inside Miss Cantrell's home before. From the outside, the Lodge Gate cottage had always struck Megan as an odd little house. For a start, it had eight sides. Every angle in it seemed offset from the next. It was a motley collection of gables and peaks, dormer windows and chimney pots. Megan thought of it as a 'house that Jack built'.

Inside the cottage, Megan's first impression was that all the furniture was much too big. It reminded her of a dolls' house with the miniature fixtures and fittings made to the wrong scale.

Each piece was of the very best quality and finest craftsmanship, and it was obviously all very old. The wood was carved, the metal wrought, the fabrics heavy and ornate. But in the small rooms of the cottage it was overwhelming.

Megan could only guess what it must have looked like when it was displayed in the huge rooms of Bartlemere Hall, with their high ceilings, massive fireplaces and big windows.

Here, out of place and crammed in, they made the cottage look poky and overfull.

The criss-cross pattern in the glass of the tiny windows added to the claustrophobic feeling.

Megan accepted Miss Cantrell's invitation to sit down. She perched her bottom on the very edge of a large, padded armchair covered in faded red velvet.

Miss Cantrell and Mrs Pleeth went into the kitchen together to unpack the pie.

Megan looked around the crowded little room. There was not a speck of dust anywhere. Whoever cleaned for Miss Cantrell had to meet high standards. The hearth was swept clean, the brass fire-tongs were polished, and the grate had been black-leaded until it gleamed.

Above, on the mantelpiece, stood an old fashioned clock with a huge glass dome. Megan jumped as the clock started to make a noise. It was a metallic, whirring sound. It stopped as suddenly as it had started and then the clock began to chime.

It was the most beautiful, sweet, bell-like sound. Megan sat and counted ten strokes. The clock face was decorated with painted flowers. Megan would have liked to get up and look at it more closely, but she didn't dare.

Mrs Pleeth came into the room carrying two cups of tea. She put one down on a dainty table beside what Megan guessed must be Miss Cantrell's favourite chair. She put the other one down beside her own seat.

Miss Cantrell followed her in with a glass of rather watery-looking lemonade for Megan.

"Thank you."

Megan received a brief nod from Miss Cantrell in response. Didn't she ever smile?

Megan sipped her lemonade, which tasted better than it looked, and listened with only half an ear to the adults' conversation.

Mrs Pleeth was telling Miss Cantrell the outcome of Mr Martin's interrogation by the police.

Megan looked out of the window. From where she was sitting she could see a view of Bartlemere Hall that you couldn't see when you walked by.

The Lodge Gate cottage garden was tidy, but beyond it the grounds of The Hall looked neglected and overgrown. They looked like a jungle.

Megan wondered how Miss Cantrell must feel, living like this, so close to her old home while it was closed up and empty.

When Mrs Pleeth had finished her tea, the conversation came to an end. Megan watched for her cue to get up, ready to leave.

Miss Cantrell saw them to the door.

"Thank you so much for coming."

"I'll see you again soon," Mrs Pleeth assured her.

"Thank you for my drink of lemonade. It was very nice."

Mrs Pleeth smiled at Megan, pleased that she had remembered her manners without being prompted. From Miss Cantrell there was just the usual, brief nod of acknowledgement.

"Why is she always so miserable?" Megan asked as they walked back across The Common. "She never smiles. I don't think she likes children."

"Miss Cantrell is a difficult lady to get to know," Mrs Pleeth explained. "She's a very shy person. I know she can appear stuck-up, and folks say she puts on airs and graces, but that is because she feels very uncomfortable around people. I've known her a long time and she's never been any different. Even when she gets to know you, she always keeps that little distance."

"That's not very nice."

"It's the way she was brought up. As a child her father taught her that the Cantrells were superior and shouldn't mix with ordinary people. If you're shy to start with, and you've had that dinned into you, you have a mountain to climb to make friends."

"I'm not surprised she never got married."

"Don't fly to judgement, Megan. Miss Cantrell was engaged to be married."

"Really?" Megan was amazed.

"Oh, yes."

"Why didn't she?"

"He died. He was sent out to South Africa as a young officer to fight in the first Boer war and was killed in action. Miss Cantrell was eighteen. That very same year her older sister died during childbirth and a year after that she lost her mother. She had a tragic young life really, Megan. A lot of people that she loved died."

"What happened to her sister's baby?"

"It was a little boy. They called him Cedric. Miss Cantrell idolised him. Her father lived to a good age and when he died, Cedric inherited Bartlemere Hall. I think that was probably the happiest time in Miss Cantrell's life. When the first war broke out, Cedric volunteered, of course. He became a Major in the British Army."

"Is that his photo, on the mantelpiece near the clock?"

"That's right."

"What happened to him?"

"He was killed at the Battle of the Somme in July 1916. I'll never forget the day the telegram arrived."

"You worked at The Hall, didn't you?"

"Yes, I was lady's maid to Miss Cantrell at the time. She fainted when she read the news. Then she took to her bed, wouldn't eat, wouldn't speak, wouldn't see any visitors. I've never seen anyone so overcome. I feared for her, I really did. I was only a young girl myself, barely seventeen. I never left her side, day or night, for weeks. She's never forgotten that. That crisis broke down the barriers between us like nothing else could have done. When I married Walter, four years later, she gave me a lovely wedding gift.

"So don't think too unkindly of her, Megan. For all her proud manners, she's a sad, lonely old lady, with no family and few friends."

CHAPTER 28

Megan was getting fed up with Mrs Pleeth keeping an eye on every move she made. After lunch she decided to ask if she could go out to play with her friends.

She half expected Mrs Pleeth to say no, but she didn't – she said Megan could go, so she set off straight away.

She started walking along the road towards Millie's house, then, because that would mean walking past Mr Hains' cottage, she changed her mind and decided to go and see Kathleen instead.

Out of habit, she looked both ways before she crossed the road, although a car in Bartlemere was such a rare event that it really wasn't necessary to look.

She cut across The Common and set off up the long track to the farm. Halfway to the house she met Kathleen and Ruth walking towards her.

Kathleen told her they had been invited to Millie's house to play until teatime, so Megan joined them and together they strolled back across The Common.

When they arrived, the girls decided to hold a dolls' tea party on the corner of The Common near Millie's house.

They settled down on the grass not far from Miss Cantrell's cottage and Megan was sure she could see the gaunt, black figure watching them from the front window.

What Mrs Pleeth had told her had made her feel quite sorry for Miss Cantrell, and how lonely she must be. She raised her arm and waved to her. There was no answering wave from the window. Perhaps Miss Cantrell hadn't seen her.

After the tea party the girls decided to make daisy chains. There were daisies growing in the grass all over The Common. They roamed about for ages gathering them, and then sat down in a ring and began making their chains. They had to make a tiny hole in each stalk and then thread the next daisy through it. It was a task only small fingers could do.

Making a daisy chain was a slow job, and it was all too easy to break the daisy's stem by accident. The game was to see who could make the longest chain. Then you could wear it round your neck like a necklace, or if it wasn't long enough for that, you could put it round your head.

Megan looked up from what she was doing and stretched. She had been sitting still for too long. Suddenly, she noticed a piece of brown wrapping paper lying nearby. It was only quite a small piece but still, wrapping paper was so hard to come by that it was worth picking up and taking home.

Millie spotted it at the same time and they both jumped up and ran to grab it.

Just as they got there, a gust of wind took it and they ran after it, laughing. Ruth and Kathleen got up and joined in the chase.

The paper seemed to have a mind of its own as it fluttered on the breeze, first this way and then that, the girls darting after it, trying to be the first to catch it.

Megan's fingers closed on one corner of the paper and she held it aloft.

"Mine! I win!" She folded her prize and stuffed it into her pocket as she ran off across the grass, back to the daisies.

Megan went back to Mere House for her tea. When she went up to her room to wash and brush up, she realised she was still wearing her daisy chain, and the wrapping paper was still in her pocket. She draped the daisy chain across the washstand. Then she took out the wrapping paper and unfolded it.

Both edges were roughly torn with jagged, dark blotches along them. The paper was blank. She turned it over and there was writing on the other side. It said:

c/o Mr Hains

Forge Cottage

Bartlemere

Megan's heart skipped a beat.

She looked again at the dark edges of the paper. Was she imagining it, or could they be burn marks?

She went and knocked at the door of her brother's room. No answer. She opened the door and peeped inside. The room was empty.

At that moment Mrs Pleeth called up the stairs.

"Come along, Megan! What's keeping you? Your tea's out on the table and we're all waiting for you!"

Megan had completely forgotten about going down for tea. Her discovery had driven everything else from her mind.

She ran back into her room and quickly washed her hands and then hurried down to the dining room.

Megan couldn't get through her tea fast enough. Eating the Spam fritters seemed to take forever. Mr Pleeth came back for second helpings. John kept serving himself with more homemade chutney. Mrs Pleeth handed round the bread and butter time after time.

All Megan wanted was to show John the piece of paper she had found and get him to examine it with his magnifying glass.

At last the meal was finished and she was allowed to leave the table. She was in such a hurry to help with the clearing away that she dropped a plate. Luckily it was in the dining room and it landed on the mat. If it had fallen on to the quarry tiled scullery floor it would certainly have smashed.

Mrs Pleeth must have feared for the rest of her crockery, because she let Megan off drying up.

Megan shot upstairs and brought the wrapping paper into her brother's room.

"Look what I found today on The Common."

"What is it?"

"I think it could be off Mr Hains' package that blew up."

John took the paper from her and looked at it closely.

"See that brown stain on the edge?" Megan asked. "Can you tell what it is?"

John reached into the drawer and got out his magnifying glass. He took the paper over to the window sill and smoothed it out as much as he could. Then he put the magnifying glass to his eye, adjusted the distance to see most clearly, and began a detailed examination of the paper.

"I think," he began, moving the glass slowly across the paper, "that the brown bits on the edges are scorch marks."

"So that could be a burn from when it exploded?"

"Quite likely."

John straightened his back and pointed down at the address written on the paper.

"It says 'C stroke O, Mr Hains, Forge Cottage, Bartlemere,'" Megan read. "What does C stroke O mean?"

"It means 'care of'. Which tells us this package wasn't intended for Mr Hains. It was sent 'care of' him, but it wasn't for him."

"So who was it for? Mrs Pleeth told me he's got a daughter. Perhaps it was for her."

"Look above that top line of writing, along the torn edge of the paper." John handed Megan the magnifying glass. She took it and moved the glass until the writing stood out clearly.

"I can see some more writing there, only I can't see what it says. It's torn right across the words."

"Can you work out what the letters are?"

Megan studied the writing as hard as she could.

"No, I can't. There's not enough writing there to tell."

Megan handed the paper and magnifying glass back to her brother.

"Meg, somehow we've got to try and find out what that top line of writing said."

CHAPTER 29

John put his magnifying glass away and they both set off downstairs and out of the house to search The Common for the rest of the wrapping paper.

"Let's go back to where you were when you found the first piece," John suggested.

Megan looked round. "I can't remember where I was."

"Were you anywhere near Mr Hains' cottage?"

"I don't think so. But it was windy. The paper was blowing about and we ran after it. The other bit could be anywhere."

They hunted everywhere but couldn't find any more scraps of wrapping paper. Eventually they gave up and went home.

Next day Megan set about a systematic search of The Common. She started after breakfast at the corner nearest Mere House and worked her way along the edge of the grass, towards the church. Then she turned to face back the way she had come, took a pace to her left and walked all the way back again.

She went back and forth, between the main road and the path that ran past the school and the farm, never taking her eyes from the ground.

She spent the whole morning criss-crossing The Common in this way, combing every tuft of grass.

At midday she went back to Mere House for her lunch. Up in her room she emptied out her pockets. She had picked up three hair slides, half-a-dozen marbles, two yellow fivestones, a wing broken off a toy aeroplane and a yo-yo, but no paper.

Where could she look next? The previous day they had chased the piece of wrapping paper quite a long way but not in a straight line. The wind had blown it zigzag, almost in a circle. The wind was still blowing today. Anything caught by a gust could go anywhere.

She wandered outside again after lunch and this time made her way towards The Mere. There was always the chance that the piece of paper had blown into the water.

She walked along the bank, past the ducking stool, towards the church, keeping her eyes on the surface of the water.

Not far from the edge, a small floating island of debris caught her eye. An assortment of leaves, ducks' feathers and small pieces of litter had been blown together by the wind.

Megan looked around until she found a long, thin twig on the ground and began poking at the collection of objects, trying to tease them apart so she could see if one of them was the vital piece of paper she was looking for.

"Be careful, Megan!" It was Miss Nicholls' voice.

Megan turned and looked up.

"Hello, Miss Nicholls!" She dropped her twig, and scrambled up the bank.

"You shouldn't be playing near the water, you know."

"It's all right. I was looking for something, but it isn't there. I'll go back and look on The Common again."

"That's a good girl."

Megan fell into step with Miss Nicholls and walked with her along the path.

"Are you enjoying your summer holidays, Miss Nicholls?"

"To be truthful, Megan, I'm afraid I'm not. My mother's not at all well, so I'm not having much of a holiday."

"Oh dear, what's the trouble?"

"She was taken ill on Monday."

"I'm really sorry. What's the matter with her?"

"She suffers from her heart, you know. And she's not getting any younger. And always having to be in a wheelchair doesn't help. She finds it very difficult."

Megan thought Miss Nicholls looked a lot more worried and anxious than she usually did.

"I hope she's better soon."

"Thank you, Megan. Look, I was just going to post this letter. You wouldn't take it across to the post box for me, would you? Then I won't have to leave her."

"Of course I will."

"Thank you so much, dear." Miss Nicholls handed Megan the letter and turned back to her cottage.

Megan took the letter and sped off towards the post box outside Mr Porter's shop.

Once the letter was safely posted, she decided to walk back to tell Miss Nicholls that she had completed her errand.

Megan had her hand on the garden gate of Miss Nicholls' cottage when she heard a voice through the open window. Miss Nicholls was speaking and she sounded upset. Megan hesitated.

"I don't know how you could, mother! Without saying a word."

Mrs Danson must have replied, but Megan didn't hear what she said. Miss Nicholls' voice was trembling when she spoke again.

"Your diamond brooch, your pearl earrings, your fur coat, your silver-topped walking stick. And now I find you've got rid of the Royal Doulton dinner service."

There was a pause. Megan presumed Mrs Danson was speaking. Miss Nicholls sounded quite sharp when she replied.

"Really, mother, you shouldn't be thinking of disposing of your belongings, yet. You've got years ahead of you, I'm sure."

Another reply, too quiet for Megan's ears to catch. Miss Nicholls' tone was softer when she spoke again, almost pleading.

"They were valuable things, mother. I wish you'd discussed it with me first."

There was a break when Mrs Danson must have spoken again. Then Megan heard Miss Nicholls once more, this time sounding near to tears.

"I really wish you hadn't sold them. They were family heirlooms."

Megan felt awful. Although she had only overheard half the conversation, it was obvious Miss Nicholls and her mother had been arguing.

She was sure Miss Nicholls would never have spoken like that if she had realised anyone was listening.

Megan hadn't intended to snoop. She hoped Miss Nicholls wouldn't suddenly look round and see that she was right outside the window.

Megan took her hand off the gate, turned, and walking as quietly as she could, retraced her steps down the path.

CHAPTER 30

Megan reported to her brother that evening that she'd had no success in finding any more of the wrapping paper. She said nothing about what she'd overheard at Miss Nicholls' cottage. She felt embarrassed about mentioning a quarrel between Miss Nicholls and Mrs Danson.

John suggested that the piece of paper might have blown into a hedge.

After tea they went out looking again, armed with a brown paper carrier bag each. John spent an hour combing the hedges along the main road outside people's houses, while Megan walked the length of the hedge near the school and the farm.

They came home with all manner of small bits of rubbish in their bags but not the elusive piece of wrapping paper.

"I must say, it's very public spirited of you to go out picking up litter," Mr Pleeth remarked.

They accepted his challenge to a game of dominoes before bedtime and settled down to play at the dining room table, while Mrs Pleeth sat doing her knitting and listening to the wireless.

Saturday morning John went to work as usual and Megan helped Mrs Pleeth with the chores. The chickens were fed, the kitchen was tidied, Mrs Pleeth's daily batch of homemade bread was set to rise in the larder.

Megan was on the lookout every moment for the postman and was delighted when he delivered a large envelope from their mother containing a knitting pattern for Mrs Pleeth and a letter for Megan and John. Megan ran upstairs to read it. Her mother was reassuring about the dramatic events in the village. She was sure everything would turn out all right. They were not to worry. Mummy's own news was about a trip to the pictures with some of her friends from work.

When Mrs Pleeth called her to come down she popped the letter in her drawer to show John later.

"I've just got a couple of errands for you, Meg. I want you to call at Mr Porter's. I've written a shopping list. There's not a lot to get today. Here's a string bag and a little purse with the money. Put that and the ration books in the bag. And one more thing. Either before you go to the shop or after, I'd like you to call at Miss Cantrell's and collect the pie dish we left there on Thursday."

"All right, Mrs Pleeth. I'll be as quick as I can."

Megan decided she would go to Miss Cantrell's first, so she wouldn't have to carry the shopping there and back again.

She crossed over on to The Common and walked across the grass. Although it was a bright sunny morning, it must have rained overnight because in no time her plimsolls were wet through.

When she reached the Lodge Gate cottage she let herself in at the garden gate and went and knocked on the front door.

Megan guessed Miss Cantrell must have seen her coming because she opened the door immediately, holding the pie dish in her hand.

Megan wondered how long she had stood watching her walking towards the house.

"Please pass on my thanks to Mrs Pleeth for her kindness. Very thoughtful of her. Please tell her I enjoyed the pie."

"Of course I will. Thank you, Miss Cantrell." Megan smiled. Again, she received just a nod in response.

Megan took the dish from the thin, lined hands and stowed it safely in the bottom of her bag. As she turned away, the front door closed behind her.

Walking back up the garden path, she noticed a scrap of paper trapped between the gate post and the fence. She reached out and pulled it free. She turned it over and glanced at it.

Yes! It was the very thing she had been searching for. She was sure of it. What a stroke of luck. In her excitement she very nearly dropped her shopping bag.

But she couldn't stand and study the paper there, in Miss Cantrell's front garden. She tucked it away safely with the ration books, and set off to the shop, hoping she could get served quickly so she could carry her prize back to Mere House.

She could hardly contain herself until John got home from work. She watched for him out of her bedroom window and as soon as she saw him coming, she ran to meet him.

"I've found it! I've found it!"

"Oh, well done, Meg! Where was it?"

"It was stuck in Miss Cantrell's fence. I only found it by accident."

"Never mind. We've got it. Can you read the name?"

"No. It's torn right across the middle. When we put the two bits together we might. But it's got stamps on it and everything."

"Come on, then! I want to have a look!"

John ran up the stairs two at a time, Megan on his heels. He went straight to the drawer in his room where he had put the original paper.

He smoothed it out on the window sill, as the had done when he first examined it. He held out his hand and Megan passed him the piece from Miss Cantrell's fence. John carefully aligned the two edges.

"Look!"

Megan leaned close and studied the name that emerged as the two pieces of the puzzle were brought together.

"Mr C. Roseby," Megan read. "Of course, he was Mr Hains' lodger. That's why it was sent 'care of' Mr Hains."

"There's only one problem with that."

"What?"

"He wasn't lodging there on Monday, Meg. He was lodging in that hole Mr Martin dug in the churchyard. Mr Roseby was dead when that parcel was sent to him."

John's bed frame squeaked as they both sank down on the edge of it.

"It doesn't make sense."

"No, it doesn't."

They were still both sitting, lost in thought, when Mrs Pleeth called upstairs:

"Lunch is ready. Come down now, please."

CHAPTER 31

It was Mrs Pleeth's homemade vegetable soup for lunch with a thick slice of new bread. John came back for a second helping.

"How are those blisters on your hands, lad?" Mr Pleeth asked, as he passed his soup plate to his wife for more.

John held out his hands, palms up.

"All gone! Look! I don't get blisters any more. My skin's really tough now."

Back upstairs in his room, John had another good look at the new piece of wrapping paper. Megan hovered behind him, anxious for a look through the magnifying glass herself.

"It's really difficult to sort out all these postmarks," John said, straightening up. "There's certainly more than one, maybe more than two. You have a look."

Megan moved the magnifying glass steadily across the coarse brown paper. All she could make out was a splodgy mess of black lines.

"I can't read anything."

"No, it is difficult. And it's not helped, of course, that it got wet in the night. Look, I'm going to have a session with Reverend Ross again tomorrow afternoon. I'll take this with me and if possible I'll try to get a look at it under the microscope. It's so much more powerful that this little magnifying glass."

"Good idea. Are you going to tell him what it is?"

"Not yet. I don't want to set off any alarm bells until we're absolutely sure we're on the right track. Do you agree?"

Megan nodded.

Reverend Ross conducted morning service next day to another packed congregation. The only notable absentees were Mrs Danson, who was too poorly to attend, and Miss Nicholls, who had stayed at home to look after her.

In the beautiful little church there was an atmosphere of shock and disbelief that such a thing could have happened in their village.

Mr Hains had not been a particularly well-liked man but he was generally respected. A lot of the older women remembered his late wife as a friendly person, and those who had gone to the village school with his daughter had liked her.

Reverend Ross spoke about the sense of outrage that was felt throughout the whole community that such an evil deed could have been committed in their midst.

Mr Pleeth sat for a long time with his head bowed and his hands folded in his lap. Megan wondered if he was praying for guidance to help find the perpetrator.

No one had the slightest idea who might have been responsible for sending the parcel bomb to Mr Hains. There were one or two sidelong glances at Mr Martin, who completely ignored them. He sat near the front and sang out loudly when Mrs Ward struck up the hymns on the organ.

After the service the crowd outside in the churchyard took longer than usual to disperse.

People seemed not to know what to say to each other, but still wanted to linger.

Lunch at Mere House was a subdued affair. Everyone seemed bowed down by the morning's sad thoughts. When they had finished, Mr Pleeth excused himself and went to do some work in his office, and Mrs Pleeth complained of a headache and went to lie down.

John tucked the slip of wrapping paper into his top pocket as he got ready to set off for his appointment at The Rectory.

"Can't I come?" Megan was feeling thoroughly left out.

"Well, all right. But you'll have to sit quiet while I'm doing experiments with Reverend Ross. Bring something to do."

Megan picked up her Enid Blyton and tucked it under her arm. As she went out of the gate she fumbled and dropped her book. When she picked it up she noticed a tear in the dust cover so she was in quite a bad mood as she hurried along to keep up with John.

"You are going to look at those postmarks, aren't you," she urged him.

"If I can, Meg, but I can't promise. I may not get the opportunity."

"You'll have to make an opportunity."

"Meg, I can't just take over Reverend Ross's microscope and do whatever I like with it, you know."

When John followed Reverend Ross into his study, Megan tried to make herself comfortable on the settee in the sitting room. She didn't even bother to open her book. She wished Tiger was still there. It would be nice to have him to cuddle while everyone was feeling so edgy and miserable.

Reverend Ross kept popping in and out of the study, fetching a book from the bookcase, going into the kitchen, searching among newspapers on the side table. He seemed not to be concentrating much on what John was doing, which Megan hoped would mean John had been able to use the microscope for his own purposes.

At the end of an hour, Reverend Ross and John both came out of the study. Megan couldn't tell from John's expression whether he had been successful or not, but before they went he did ask Reverend Ross if he could look in one of his books.

"Do you have a gazetteer of the British Isles I could look in, please. I just want to look up a place name."

"Of course, John. No problem at all. It's over here."

Reverend Ross fetched it from the bottom shelf of the bookcase and John quickly scanned the index and then turned to one of the map pages. He was done in a moment and handed the book back with a polite 'thank you'. Reverend Ross didn't ask what place John was interested in. He simply thanked them for coming and saw them on their way, seeming to Megan quite pleased to close the door behind them.

"Did you do it?" she hissed at her brother as they walked down the garden path. He nodded, but, until they were well away from The Rectory, John wouldn't tell her anything.

Once back home and in his room, John got out the paper and his magnifying glass and tried to show Megan, as best he could, what he had been able to see so clearly under the microscope.

"There are actually three postmarks with three separate dates. The top one is a London mark. It's smudged but I think it says 'London L.P.O.' The date on that is the 7th of July. The one under that says Bartlestone, dated the 22nd of May."

"Bartlestone – where's that?"

"Wait a minute, I'm coming to that. The original postmark is Market Hampton on May the first."

"May – but we're in the middle of July. Where's it been all that time?"

"I can only guess, but this is what I think might have happened. Mr Roseby was very much alive on the first of May and it looks as if someone sent the parcel to him from Market Hampton then, expecting him to get it a few days later.

"Of course, we know it didn't arrive. It seems to have been misdirected by mistake to Bartlestone instead of Bartlemere.

"I looked Bartlestone up on the map and it's right on the other side of the country, hundreds of miles away. Well, obviously they couldn't deliver it, but they don't seem to have been in any hurry to send it on to the right address. It stayed in Bartlestone until 22nd of May.

"Now, why it went to London I don't know, but going by this postmark, that's where the Bartlestone post office sent it."

"Let me look," Megan held out her hand for the wrapping paper. Although she couldn't read the smudged postmarks she felt she could think better if she had the paper in her hand. "Did you say those letters were L.P.O.?"

"Yes, or something like that."

"Could that stand for 'Lost Parcels Office' do you think?"

"Megan, that's brilliant! Obviously, there was no return address on it. So that's where it went. And they seem to have forgotten about it until a week ago last Friday. And it was delivered to the right address on the Monday.

"Of course, by then Mr Roseby was dead. He didn't have any relatives to pass it on to. I suppose Mr Hains opened it just because he was curious to know what was in it."

"Curiosity killed the cat," Megan quoted.

CHAPTER 32

"What did you say?" John sprang up so quickly that Megan was quite startled.

"What did I say what?"

"About the cat – curiosity killed the cat."

"Well, it's a saying. I only said it because you said Mr Hains was curious."

"I know, but the cat part – maybe there's a connection."

"What are you talking about, John?"

"Tiger! Meg, what if the same person who killed Mr Hains killed Tiger?"

"But Mr Hains was sent a bomb and Tiger was poisoned." It didn't seem to Megan that the two deaths had anything in common.

"But now we know the bomb wasn't intended for Mr Hains. He was just the innocent victim. It was Mr Roseby who should have been blown up. I don't think anyone ever meant to poison Tiger, he just ate that cream cake by accident."

"Reverend Ross said Mr Roseby gave him the cake."

"But Mr Roseby wasn't trying to poison Reverend Ross. He just didn't like the flavour. He didn't know the cake had been tampered with. He told Reverend Ross someone had given it to him."

"The person who had tried to kill him before, with the bomb?"

"Exactly. Mr Roseby was the one who should have eaten the poison. So Tiger is a link. When was he killed?"

"What date is it today?"

"The 16th of July."

Megan started working it out.

"Reverend Ross told us about it when we first got here, at the end of June. He said it was about a month before that. So that would make it about the last week of May or the first week of June."

"Right, Meg. And the bomb was originally sent on May the first, according to the Market Hampton postmark."

"So when the person who sent the bomb realised that Mr Roseby never got it, they gave it a month and then they tried again with something else."

"I believe so."

They both sat quietly for a moment, thinking over what their discovery meant.

"What date did Mr Roseby actually die, Meg?"

"The 26th of June."

"It looks as if the same thing happened again. When Mr Roseby didn't die of poisoning, the killer waited a few weeks and then tried again with something different. And that time it worked."

"Third time lucky."

"You're full of sayings today, Meg. It wasn't very lucky for Mr Roseby."

"Sorry, I didn't mean that. But, you know, if someone was that determined to kill him, I think even if he'd survived falling in The Mere, they would have found a way sooner or later."

"Why would anybody go to such lengths to see Mr Roseby dead?"

"They must have really hated him."

"Meg, this is a single-minded killer. They have to be caught."

"What can we do?"

"The first thing is to convince people that Mr Roseby's death wasn't an accident. While ever they think the chain on the ducking stool just broke, the police won't even be looking for a murderer."

"So we need to find that chain. If it turns out to be sawn through, that will prove it was intentional."

"Yes."

"How did you get on with working out where it would be?"

"It's an awfully complicated calculation but if I'm right, it's in the water at the foot the tree opposite the ducking stool."

"Let's go fishing, then." Megan was up and heading for the door.

John laughed.

"We need to go prepared. It's a metal chain. It will have sunk to the bottom. The only way I can think of to pull it out is with a magnet."

"You'll need a big, strong magnet, then. Your little one won't do it, will it?

"No. But Mr Martin's got one that might."

"Shall we go and see him tomorrow night, then, after tea?"

"All right."

On Monday evening John led the way to the yard at the back of Mr Martin's cottage. Mr Martin was sorting through some scrap metal.

"Well, bless me if I haven't got visitors again. How are you two young mischief-makers today?"

John got straight to the point.

"Mr Martin, do you remember showing me a great big magnet? You used to keep it hanging up in your workshop. Have you still got it?"

"I think it's about, somewhere, John."

"Can you find it?"

"I might, if you two help me look."

"Come on, Meg, help us. We're looking for a big magnet. It's shaped like a horseshoe and about this big." John held his hands out to show the size.

"If it's a magnet, won't it be stuck to something metal?"

Mr Martin laughed.

"You're quick, young Megan. That's the reason I used to keep it hanging up."

Mr Martin left what he was doing and led them into his workshop. Megan picked her way through all the junk, on full spider alert. John headed off towards the far wall.

"Might it be over here on the bench, Mr Martin?"

Mr Martin followed John and began picking things up and turning them over and putting them down again.

"So why have you got a magnet in mind today, me lad?"

"I wondered if I might borrow it, please?"

"O'course you can, if we ever find it. What you goin' to do with it?"

"Some more experiments. You know I told you about my notebook where I write down all my experiments?"

"I remember. Well, let's poke around a bit more. It's sure to be here somewhere."

Megan didn't think they stood a chance of finding anything. She wandered off out of the workshop and back into the yard. She took a long, careful look round the yard and at the outside of the workshop.

Something hanging up inside one of the cobweb-covered windows caught her eye. It was a big silver horseshoe-shape with the ends painted red. She went and stuck her head back inside the workshop.

"Found it!"

John scrambled up to get the magnet while Mr Martin held on to his legs.

"Thanks so much, Mr Martin."

"Oh, you thank that little sister of yours. She spotted it. Smart girl, that one."

Mr Martin waved them on their way with a smile.

When they got the magnet home John insisted they did some experiments with it to see how much weight it would hold.

"It's a really strong one, Meg. Look at how much you can pick up with it."

"We'd better make sure we use really strong string, then. We don't want to fish out the chain and then watch it fall back into the water because the string breaks."

CHAPTER 33

"Where are we going to get strong string?"

"There's loads up at the farm. That thick, coarse string they use for baling up. I can get some of that. And we'll need something to make a fishing rod, too. I'll see what I can find. There's always stuff lying about that I can borrow. I'll bring some home tomorrow night."

John was as good as his word, and on Tuesday night he arrived home with some string and a pole in an empty potato sack. Megan helped him tie the string round the top of the magnet and knot it really tightly. They fixed the other end of the string to the pole.

"So are we going on this magnetic fishing trip after dinner, Meg?"

"Okay. We'll tell Mrs Pleeth we're going out for a walk."

When the time came, John bundled the magnet and string into the sack and carried it in his arms, with the pole sticking out over his shoulder.

"Don't let Mrs Pleeth see that lot. She'll start asking questions."

"Don't worry, she's out in the back garden."

Megan hurried along beside him.

"Do try not to look so guilty, Meg. You'll make people think we're up to no good."

Megan laughed.

"If anyone does see us messing around at The Mere they'll make us go home."

But their luck held. They didn't meet anybody on their short walk across the road.

They skirted round to the willow tree that grew on the very edge of The Mere, on the opposite side to the ducking stool. Half its roots grew in the bank and half in the water. There was quite a lot of undergrowth round the bottom of the tree. They did their best to keep out of sight there while they unpacked the rod and magnet.

"Now what, John?"

"Just throw the magnet in, I suppose, and drag it back towards us and see if anything's stuck to it when we pull it out of the water."

"Okay."

John threw the magnet as hard as he could. It made such a splash, it made them both jump. They looked anxiously around, expecting someone to come to see what was going on, but no one disturbed them.

The magnet hadn't gone very far from the bank. Pulling it in was hard work because the bank sloped steeply and there was nowhere to get a good foothold. When they did manage to get it out, there was nothing clinging to it.

"That's not much good. Can't you throw it any further?"

John changed tactics. Next time, instead of simply throwing the magnet, he held it flat and skimmed it over the water, to get it to go further.

"That's better."

There was still nothing sticking to it when they pulled it out.

John had several more goes, all without success.

A sudden thought struck Megan.

"I hope it doesn't land on any fish and kill them."

John burst out laughing.

"I'm sorry, but it's their hard luck if they don't swim out of the way in time."

"But be careful, anyway."

"Meg, I can't see any fish, so I can't try to miss them. Anyway, it's hard enough throwing this thing without trying to aim it anywhere in particular. Do you want to have a go?"

Megan didn't.

John crouched down and threw the magnet again.

They had no means of hauling it in except raising the rod upright and pulling on the line. Very soon, the coarse, wet string had scratched Megan's hands raw.

She squatted by the water, gritted her teeth and said nothing as John tried again and again. It looked as if there wasn't anything metal in The Mere, or if there was, they were looking in the wrong place.

Either way, she was not going to be the one to say when it was time to give up and go home.

At last, John admitted defeat.

"What do you think, Meg? Shall we call it a day? We're getting nowhere, are we?"

"Don't seem to be."

John stood up and stretched.

He leaned the fishing rod up against the tree and reached a hand out to Megan to pull her to her feet.

"Sorry to drag you out here for nothing, Meg."

"No, no. I wanted to come. We said we'd do this together. It's not your fault we haven't found anything."

John leaned back against the trunk of the willow.

"I'm sure my calculations were right. If the broken chain was flung in the air when the ducking stool went down, this has to be where it landed. I've tried in every direction out from the bank. I can't understand why it isn't here."

"Give it one more go, for luck."

John smiled down at his sister.

"Okay. Pass me the rod."

When Megan picked up the rod, the string had got tangled round it. She flicked it, to free it, but that didn't work. She flicked it again, much harder. To her annoyance the magnet whipped upwards and caught on the trunk of the tree, just out of reach.

"Sorry. I didn't mean to do that."

"Your trouble is, you don't know your own strength," John laughed at her.

He stepped forward to help. He took the rod and yanked at it, trying to get the magnet down.

The magnet was only caught on a twig and with his second jerk it came free and fell down at his feet.

"Look out!" Megan pulled him aside.

It seemed the magnet wasn't all he'd pulled free. Something long and snake-like came slithering out of the branches. It landed on the magnet with a metallic clang.

"Meg! Look! It's the chain!"

"So, you were right. Only it went into the tree instead of down in the water."

"It just didn't occur to me that it might hit the tree. How could I have been so stupid?"

"Never mind. We've got it. That's all that matters. Well done!"

John gathered up the fishing rod as Meg put the chain in the potato sack.

They walked back to Mere House as fast as they could.

Megan stayed in the kitchen while John ran upstairs to stash everything in the back of his wardrobe.

Mrs Pleeth came through from the dining room.

"Mrs Pleeth, I've hurt my hands. Could I have some Germolene, please?"

"Let me have a look."

Mrs Pleeth inspected Megan's hands, shaking her head. "There you go, falling over and grazing yourself again, Megan. Do try to be more careful in future, dear."

She went to fetch the ointment and dabbed it onto Megan's palms.

"I'll try to be careful, Mrs Pleeth. Thank you for putting the stuff on. Goodnight."

John called down the stairs.

"Goodnight, Mrs Pleeth."

"Goodnight to you both."

Mrs Pleeth went back to her knitting as Megan went up to her room.

CHAPTER 34

The children both got undressed and ready for bed, then Megan went and tapped quietly on John's door. He quickly let her in and shut the door behind her. He fetched the potato sack from his wardrobe and tipped the chain out on to the floor.

They both crouched down beside it, studying it.

The chain was black. The strong-looking links were made of metal the thickness of Megan's thumbs. Each link was an identical, smooth oval shape that looped perfectly through the next. It was so finely made that it was impossible to see where the joins were in the metal.

Part way along its length, two links, which must have been the original ends of the chain, were joined by a hefty padlock.

John took hold of the padlock and gave it a sharp pull. The padlock held firm, with no sign of being loose or damaged.

"Nothing the matter with that. It's as good as new."

He turned his attention to the chain. Megan examined it with him.

"It looks really solid."

"I agree, Meg. Although it's old, the metal doesn't look to be worn out."

"So what are we looking for?"

"One of the links could have weakened with age until it finally went pop. Can you see a twisted link?"

"No. The only one that's broken is this one at the end. But it isn't twisted. If you could push the two ends back together again, they would fit perfectly."

John took the chain and looked at it under his magnifying glass.

"That link never came apart on its own. Look, you can see saw marks."

John breathed on his magnifying glass and polished it on his pyjama sleeve and handed it to Megan.

She held it over the chain until she got the focus right over the final link. At the two raw edges, silver metal showed clearly through the black."

"Are those silver marks where it was sawn through?"

"Yes."

Megan put the magnifying glass down.

"And the chain still held the ducking stool down until Mr Roseby put his weight on it?"

"Yes."

Megan suddenly had an idea.

"I wonder what happened to the saw."

"Good thought, Meg!"

"We ought to look for it."

"After they'd finished with it they probably threw it in The Mere."

"We could try and get it out with the magnet."

"Hang on a minute, Meg. The Mere's big. We've no idea where to fish for it, even if it's in The Mere at all."

"Where else can we look?"

"It could be absolutely anywhere. Think how we searched and searched for that bit of wrapping paper."

"Well, if it could be absolutely anywhere, then starting with The Mere is as good anything."

"Okay. But if we do find a saw in the water, how could we be sure it's the right one? Anyone could have thrown an old saw in there."

Megan closed her eyes and tried hard to think.

"The chain's made of metal. Would they have had to use a special saw to cut through it?"

"Good girl, Megan! Probably, yes. To cut through a chain as thick as that."

"So we need to look for a special metal-cutting saw. Where can we find out about saws?"

"We'll have to go back and talk to Mr Martin again."

There was no chance to go the following day because it was Mr Hains' funeral.

The whole thing was in marked contrast to Mr Roseby's funeral, a fortnight before. The church was crowded and a get-together had been announced at The Man in the Moon afterwards.

Megan stared at the back view of the tall, slim woman in a navy blue uniform in the front pew.

"Is that Mr Hains' daughter?" she asked Mrs Pleeth.

"Yes, that's his Mary."

John hadn't attended the funeral because he was at work, but Megan told him about it later.

"I felt so sorry for his daughter. She must think there's someone who has a grudge against her father, and it isn't true."

159

"We might be able to prove that, and make it right for her, Meg."

"I hope so."

After tea on Thursday they paid another call on Mr Martin.

"Hello, you two ragamuffins! Come to bring my magnet back, have you?"

"No, not yet. We'd like to keep it a bit longer, if that's okay."

"You hang on to it as long as you like, me dears."

Megan plunged straight in.

"Do you have a saw that can cut through metal, Mr Martin?"

"I do, at that. Or leastways, I did. To tell the truth, I've lost the run of my hacksaw. I did a little job at Miss Nicholls' house and I thought I might have left it there, but when I asked her she hadn't seen it. I done a repair in the toilets at The Man in the Moon but they said they hadn't got it either. I dunno. Perhaps I just dropped it out of my tool bag."

"What does it look like?"

"Well, it's not very big. The frame is made out of steel and the blade fixes across from the front to the part where the handle joins on. You can change the blade. You take the old one out and fit the new one in. They don't last long, so you need to be able to change 'em."

"Are the blades for cutting metal the same as the blades for cutting wood?"

"No, they're not. The ones for cutting metal have much smaller teeth. You wouldn't get far trying to saw through metal with a wood saw."

"How long would it take you to cut through a piece of metal that thick?" Megan held out her thumb.

"Well, that all depends."

"On what?"

"Well, in me workshop, with the object clamped in a vice on the bench, and a new blade in me saw, I'd say about five minutes."

"Is that all?"

"Yes, but if I was working somewhere awkward where I'd nothing to hold the thing steady, and me blade wasn't sharp, that's a different matter. It could take me half an hour."

"I see. Thank you."

Mr Martin looked at Megan with a smile on his face.

"You thinking of setting up as an odd job man in competition with me, young lady?"

Megan laughed.

"No. I just wondered."

"You're a strange one and no mistake, what goes on inside that pretty little head of yours!" Mr Martin beamed at her.

They said goodbye to Mr Martin shortly afterwards.

"Something's puzzling me," Megan said as they walked home. "Mr Martin said if you weren't in the workshop, it could take half an hour to saw through metal that thick. Surely, somebody would have seen them doing it."

"They must have done it at night when it was dark."

"It's right outside Mere House. They wouldn't have dared use a light. You know what Mr Pleeth's like about people breaking the blackout rules."

"They certainly took a chance, whenever they did it."

"Well, at least we know what kind of a saw we're looking for now, John."

"But we don't know where to look."

"I thought we'd agreed to start with The Mere."

John sighed. "All right. But I don't hold out much hope."

CHAPTER 35

After tea on Friday evening Megan and John walked across to The Mere to plan their magnetic fishing trip. The ducking stool was still tipped down into the water.

"I wish they'd put it back up again," Megan said. "It looks horrible like this."

John went and squatted down beside the iron hoop in the ground where the chain and padlock used to be.

"Let's pretend I'm the murderer sawing through the chain. Where am I going to throw the saw when I've finished?"

He swivelled round on his heels, looking in every direction at the margins of The Mere.

On the right-hand bank, quite near the ducking stool, there was a big old sycamore tree, almost opposite the willow where they had found the chain. Like the willow, it was surrounded by undergrowth and had roots sticking out into the water.

"There!" They both said it at once.

"It's the obvious place," Megan said.

John led the way round the water's edge. They got as close as they could to the tall-growing undergrowth around the base of the sycamore tree. The branches were thick. They cast shadows over the water below. In the depths, they could see a tangle of reeds and waterweed.

"It's the perfect place," Megan said. "That's where I'd chuck something I didn't want to be found."

"That's going to be our problem, Meg. Finding something as small as a saw in there won't be easy."

"We've got the magnet."

"Yes, but I'm not sure we'll be able to get the magnet right down to the bottom. There's a lot of plants growing under the water that it could get snarled up on. It was different on the other side of The Mere where we were fishing for the chain. The magnet just dropped straight to the bottom there."

"But we're going to try anyway, aren't we?"

"I suppose so. It's the most likely place the saw will be."

"Tomorrow night, then."

"Okay." John reluctantly agreed.

The following morning, when she went out after breakfast, Megan saw Mr Martin across the road, beside the ducking stool. To her surprise, John and another of the farmhands were walking across The Common towards him. They were carrying an extending ladder.

"You're going to get your wish, Meg. We're bringing the ducking stool up," John told her when she went over to him. "Mr Fairbrother sent me and Pete to help."

Word had spread like wildfire and by the time Mr Martin was ready to start work he had an audience of village children and quite a few adults.

First, he and the boys adjusted the ladder until it was extended as far as it would go. Then Mr Martin propped it up against the arm of the ducking stool, which was sticking up into the sky.

With John and Pete holding the ladder steady, they watched Mr Martin climb carefully up with a coil of rope around his shoulder. When he reached the top he slipped one end of the rope through the loop at the end of the arm, and pushed a long length of it through. Pete caught hold of it, while John still steadied the ladder. Mr Martin kept the rest of the rope round his shoulder. Then he carefully climbed back down again. When he was back on the ground, Pete handed Mr Martin the end of the rope that was attached to the ducking stool.

The two boys got busy folding the ladder up again.

Mr Martin took the coil of rope off his shoulder and peered upwards. The middle of the rope was through the loop on the ducking stool and he was holding both long ends. He gripped a handful of each end and pulled. The people watching could see the rope taking the strain through the loop up above, but for a moment nothing moved.

Then, very gradually, the end of the ducking stool that was under the water started to rise.

"Come and give me a hand, you two!" Mr Martin got Pete on one end of the rope and John on the other while he kept a hand on each, and with their combined strength they managed to slowly pull the submerged end of the ducking stool out of The Mere.

The water ran streaming off it as it came up into the sunshine, and the watching crowd cheered.

"Keep pulling until the arm's level," Mr Martin instructed. They did so, and then with another combined heave they brought the dry end down as the wet end went up.

The dry end came nearer and nearer to the ground. Mr Martin was able to get hold of loop on the end of it. He and John held on to that while Pete put the ends of the rope through the iron staple in the ground.

"Well done, lads! Now, you hold that there while I put this 'ere chain through." In a moment the chain was attached and fastened with a padlock as big and solid as the one Megan knew had been used before.

Megan watched Pete pull the rope out from the iron hoop. As he coiled it up again, Pete checked the rope. One end was in good condition but the other end was coming unravelled. Pete got out his pocket knife and cut off the last few inches of the damaged rope. Megan saw him put his knife back in his trouser pocket and toss the unwanted end of the rope into The Mere. It went into the water among the tangle of undergrowth below the sycamore tree. Exactly where they had predicted the murderer would have thrown the saw.

CHAPTER 36

On Saturday John had to work all day. The harvest was in full swing and all hands were needed every available hour. He came home at teatime starving hungry and not wanting to do anything after he had eaten, except flop on the settee and read a book. Megan didn't even mention saw-hunting.

After morning church on Sunday, and a visit to Reverend Ross in the afternoon for more experiments with the microscope, John shut himself in his room with his notebook and said he didn't want to be disturbed. Megan thought he was probably having a sleep.

It was after tea on Monday when Megan mentioned their fishing trip again.

"Please, John. You said we could do it."

"Oh, all right, I suppose so."

He collected the sack from his wardrobe and when they were sure Mrs Pleeth wasn't looking out of the window, they went across to The Mere. They made straight for the undergrowth round the base of the big sycamore tree.

John got the magnet out and threw it into the water. It had hardly gone down any distance when it caught on one of the jutting out tree roots. They could see it, just under the surface. John hauled on the string and managed to get the magnet back on the bank.

"Try skimming it, like you did before."

He did, but the reeds extended quite a distance from the shore and the magnet fell among them. This time, no matter how hard John tugged on the string, he couldn't dislodge it. Either the magnet or the string had got entangled in the reeds and was caught there. He struggled for five minutes but couldn't budge it.

"Can't you do it?" Megan couldn't believe her brother couldn't free the magnet.

John caught the irritation in her voice.

"Do you want to try?"

He passed the rod to Megan and she started dragging at the string, willing it to come loose and bring the magnet up to the surface, but it didn't.

"Now what are we going to do?" John took the rod back from her and tried again.

Megan watched his unsuccessful attempts.

"I think we should just jump in and get it out."

"Are you mad, Meg? That water's deep."

"How deep?"

"I don't know exactly. Probably too deep to stand up in."

"We'll have to dive down then."

"Meg, can you hear what you're saying? That'd be really dangerous."

"But we've got to get it back."

John stood four-square in front of Megan with a stern look on his face.

"I'm not diving into The Mere, even to get the magnet back."

"We've got to get it. It belongs to Mr Martin. We've got to give it back to him."

"I don't care. I'll tell him we've lost it. I'm not going in the water for it."

Megan stared at her brother.

"Are you scared?"

"Yes, if you want the truth, I am. The Mere's not fit for swimming in. You know they're always telling us we mustn't go in. There's reeds and roots and mud and all sorts you could get trapped in under the water. It's not worth taking a chance."

"I say it is. We've got to get that magnet back. Otherwise, bang goes the one chance we have of finding the saw. And that's an important piece of evidence."

"Well, I'm not going in The Mere after it."

"Okay. Then I will!"

"You jolly well won't!"

"One of us has got to go in and get it, and if it's not you, John, then it'll have to be me!"

"Meg, listen to me. We need to think this through before we do anything. You're right, the magnet's stuck and it's not going anywhere. So we can safely leave it where it is for now. We don't have to get it out at this minute."

"So when are we going to come back and get it?"

"When we've decided exactly how we're going to do it. I'm not joking, Meg, it really is dangerous to go in the water."

John climbed back up the bank and walked round the edge of The Mere, back the way they had come, and sat down on the arm of the ducking stool. Meg followed. She went to hoist herself up beside him, but her foot caught on something and she lost her balance. She looked down to see what she had tripped on.

It was the coil of rope Mr Martin had used when he righted the ducking stool. It must have fallen there and been missed when he packed away. She picked it up and showed it to John.

"There you are. You could tie that round your middle and jump in and I could hold on to the end and pull you out if you got into difficulties."

"I'd be far too heavy for you. I'd pull you in with me."

"But you could easily pull me out, couldn't you? I'd be willing to go in."

"Meg, don't be stupid!"

"I don't mind, honest I don't."

John looked at her: "That would be very brave."

"You don't think it's brave. You think it's daft!"

Megan laughed and was glad that John laughed too.

"To tell the truth, I think we're both daft, you for saying you'd go in and me for even thinking of encouraging you!"

Later that evening, when they were sure Mrs Pleeth was not watching, Megan and John crept downstairs and out of the back door of Mere House.

They made their way cautiously across the road and over to the big sycamore tree. John had the coil of rope round his shoulders. Megan had changed into her oldest clothes. She had a pair of scissors in her pocket that she usually kept in her knitting bag.

They edged as far as they could behind the trunk of the tree, well out of sight of the road. Their fishing gear was still where they had left it, with the string trailing down into the water, but the magnet had sunk out of sight.

John took the rope off his shoulder. He tied one end firmly to the nearest branch that jutted out over the water. He tugged on the rope to make sure the knot was secure and wouldn't slip undone. Then he tossed the other end over another branch, close to the trunk. He caught the end again before it went into the water and handed it to Megan. She put it round her waist and tied it in front of her.

John checked the knot. "Put your arms up."

She did so. The rope slipped up her chest but held fast under her arm pits.

"Take hold of the rope."

She grabbed it with both hands and tugged. John tugged back. He nodded.

"There, I think that will do. How does it feel?"

"Scratchy."

John shrugged. "Tell me again what you're going to do, Meg."

"Grab the magnet, cut the string and pull on the rope and you'll haul me out."

"Right. Putting the rope over this branch means I can pull you upwards, which will work a lot better than me just trying to drag you from the bank."

"Okay."

"And listen. I'm going to start counting as soon as your head goes under and when I get to twenty I'm going to pull you out, whether you've cut through the string or not."

"All right."

"Fingers crossed, Meg."

"Fingers crossed."

"Don't jump in. Just slide in down the bank. And when you get in the water, try not to kick about or you'll stir up a load of mud off the bottom."

Megan nodded. She was keen to get on with it.

"Take a big, deep breath then, and in you go."

The water was freezing as it closed over Megan's head. She hadn't expected it to be so cold on a summer day. It nearly made her gasp. She remembered just in time not to let out any of the precious air she was saving in her lungs to enable her to keep below the water as long as possible.

She had thought about taking her plimsolls off before she got in but she had been afraid there may be something horrible on the bottom that her feet might touch.

She didn't dare open her eyes.

She was surprised at how many things there were under the water that you didn't see from above. She seemed surrounded by strange-shaped objects that she couldn't identify. Could they all be bits of tree root? She felt about with her hands but she couldn't tell what she was touching. No magnet, for sure. Everything was slippery and weird and confusing.

John had been right. The pond was deep. She was relieved when at last she felt the bottom. But it wasn't solid. She lost her footing and fell forwards. The angle of the rope round her chest dragged her upright but there was nothing to hold on to and next moment she was down again.

She dangled on the end of the rope like a rag doll in the water. Panic rose up in her as she realised she no longer knew which way was up or down. Although her eyes were squeezed shut, little pinpoints of light appeared, flickering, at the edges of her vision. Her chest was hurting with a burning pain. She was going to have to breathe soon. She wouldn't be able to help it. If only this spinning would stop. Her body felt weightless, out of control, falling in a backwards somersault.

She thrust out her hands, clawing at anything to hang on to, to steady herself. One hand closed round something soft and slimy that

171

quickly slithered out of her grasp. Her other hand touched a solid object that moved through the water with her as she swung with the movement of the rope.

Moments later, her brother dragged her, choking, out of The Mere and up on to the bank beside him.

CHAPTER 37

Megan was barely conscious. She was only half-aware of John holding her as she coughed up water and bits of weed.

"Meg! Meg! Are you all right?"

John's voice sounded faint and distant. Everything was fuzzy. What did he want?

"Speak to me, Meg!" She tried to answer him, tell him she was fine, but her voice wouldn't work.

"Meg! Say something!" Her brother kept on insisting that she talk to him.

"Are you all right, Meg?"

"Umm. I'm Okay."

"Sit up, Meg." Her brother supported her as she struggled to sit up, spluttering and half crying. Her ears were full of water. She shook her head. She felt better when the water was out of her ears and she could hear properly.

"You're all right, Meg. Everything's going to be okay. Just say something to me."

"Yes. Okay." Of course she was okay. Except she felt woozy, light-headed.

"Take deep breaths," John told her.

She tried to but it made her cough. She spat out a mouthful of Mere water.

"Did I . . . ?" Speaking was such an effort.

"Yeah, yeah, you did fine. Just relax and keep taking deep breaths."

She leaned back against the trunk of the sycamore tree and did as she was told. The deep breaths helped to settle her. The dizziness gradually stopped. She opened her eyes. Things around her began to come back into focus. Little by little, she remembered where she was and what she was doing there.

"Meg, the most important thing now is to get you home. Can you stand up?"

"Umm." Megan tried but her legs buckled under her.

"Come on. I'll carry you."

John picked Megan up in his arms and hurried back across the road to Mere House. As he brought her through the open back door he lowered her gently on to her feet in the kitchen.

"Quick, Mrs Pleeth! Megan fell in The Mere!"

Mrs Pleeth was sitting at the dining room table. She jumped up in alarm and rushed to them.

"Oh my God! Is she all right?" Mrs Pleeth rushed back into the dining room and fetched a chair.

"My dear child, look at the state of you. How ever did you fall in The Mere? Haven't I told you time and again not to play near the water. Goodness me, whatever shall I say to your mother."

Mrs Pleeth's anxious scolding continued as she grabbed the roller towel from the back of the kitchen door and began rubbing at Megan's head and face.

"Get her shoes and socks off, John, there's a good boy. And put the kettle on, quickly. I'd better make you both a nice cup of tea. Then run upstairs and get me some dry clothes for her from her room. Goodness me, what a commotion."

Mrs Pleeth continued to fire off orders. John did everything he was told. Megan sat quiet and contrite, allowing herself to be alternately fussed over and told off.

The cup of tea was very welcome. It restored her spirits and she began to feel better.

The tea drunk, Mrs Pleeth decided the best thing was for Megan to go straight in the bath. More kettles and pans were put on the hob to boil.

Mrs Pleeth went out into the yard and fetched the tin bath from the nail where it hung when it was not in use.

In a very short space of time the kitchen was transformed into a bathroom. Mrs Pleeth fetched extra towels and a bath mat from the airing cupboard, then she closed the curtains and slid the bolt across on the back door.

John was despatched back upstairs with the change of clothes he had brought down and told this time to bring back pyjamas and dressing gown.

"And bring your own as well as your sister's. You're wet through yourself. When Megan's finished, you go in the bath too."

When all the water was boiling, Mrs Pleeth poured it from the kettles and pans into the bath, and then added cold water until it was a comfortable temperature for Megan to get into. Mrs Pleeth threw in a handful of soda crystals.

"Just as good as bath salts, but without the scent," she said.

Megan climbed into the bath and sat down, wallowing in the lovely hot water. She was the only person to use the bath who was small enough to stretch out in it, and even then she couldn't quite straighten her legs.

Very soon the combination of the hot bath and Mrs Pleeth's cup of tea had worked their magic, and Megan was feeling as good as new.

She got out of the bath and wrapped a towel around herself and went and tapped on the dining room door. Mrs Pleeth had more towels in there and her night clothes. She went through to put her pyjamas on, as John came into the kitchen to take his turn in the bath.

When they had both finished, Mrs Pleeth inspected them.

"I'm glad to see the pair of you looking none the worse. I dare not think of what might have happened. Megan, my girl, let this be a lesson to you not to go near The Mere again. And you pulled her out, John. You were very quick and brave. What would she have done if you hadn't seen she was in trouble. My heart was in my mouth when you came bursting into the kitchen, I can tell you. But all's well that ends well, I'm glad to say. I think you'd both best have an early night."

"Thank you, Mrs Pleeth. Goodnight." Megan went and John followed her upstairs and into her room.

"Are you sure you're okay, Meg?"

"Yes, I feel fine now, I really do. No damage done."

"Thank goodness. It's a good job Mr Pleeth isn't at home or we might have had a bit more explaining to do about why were messing about at The Mere."

"After all that, did I get the magnet out? I can't remember."

"Oh, yes, Meg. You got it out. And more."

CHAPTER 38

"What do you mean? What else did I fish out?"

"You won't believe it, Meg, but the magnet actually had a saw sticking to it."

"You're joking!"

"No. We actually caught it. Always assuming it is the right saw, of course."

"On our first try! Well done, John!"

"Well, second actually, but very nearly first. I mean, after how many goes we had trying to get the chain, it was really quick."

"But the chain wasn't in the water, John, was it? If it had been, maybe we would have got that first go, too. Anyway, we've got it. That's great."

"And that's not all we've got."

"What do you mean?"

"There was a stick attached to the saw."

"What sort of a stick?"

"Meg, I didn't look. You were hardly breathing. I was concentrating on making sure you were still alive."

"So where is it?"

"I stuffed the rope and the saw and the stick into the sack with the magnet and wedged it down among the tree roots. I'm pretty sure it can't fall back in the water."

"What happens if someone else finds it?"

"We just have to hope that they don't. As soon as we get an opportunity, we'll go and get it and have a good look at the saw and the stick."

"Tomorrow?"

"It's Sunday tomorrow. There'll be too many people about. Better leave it until Monday."

"When you get home from work?"

"After tea."

"Okay."

"Are you sure you're all right, Meg?"

"Yeah. I'm fine. But I'm ready to go to sleep now."

"Me, too."

"Goodnight, John."

"Goodnight."

On Monday evening John was late back from work, and was tired. Mrs Pleeth was concerned about him and how hard he was working. She fussed over him and gave him an extra slice of corned beef at teatime.

After the meal he wearily walked with Megan across to the sycamore tree by The Mere.

The sack was still there. John rummaged about among the tree roots and pulled it free. Then he upended it and tipped the contents on to the bank.

The small metal saw was still firmly stuck to the big magnet.

What puzzled Megan was that the saw was tied to the bottom end of a black stick.

John prized the saw off the magnet and passed it over to Megan, with the stick. Megan turned the stick upside down. It was topped with a silver knob. Megan wiped it clean with her hand and read the initials engraved in fancy letters in the silver: *E.D.*

"I know whose this is, John. I remember it from when we lived here before. I always used to think how pretty the curly letters were."

"Whose is it?"

"E.D. stands for Edith Danson. Miss Nicholls' mother. It's hers. Or rather, it was hers."

Megan had suddenly remembered the conversation she had overheard outside Miss Nicholls' cottage.

"What do you mean?"

"I heard Mrs Danson telling Miss Nicholls that she'd sold it."

"Who to?"

"She didn't say."

"Well, we've got to find out. Because whoever bought the stick, they also had the saw."

"Is it the right saw, John? I mean, is it one that would saw through metal?"

"Yes, look at these tiny teeth. I mean, I can't guarantee it's the actual saw that the murderer used, but it must have been one like this."

"So the person who bought the stick off Mrs Danson must be the murderer."

"It looks like it."

They packed everything back into the sack and John carried it home. For all their efforts, they seemed to have finished up with more questions than answers.

The following evening they went to see Mr Martin once more to take his magnet back and thank him for the loan. John climbed up to hang it back in the window for him. They didn't stay long because John had worked late again and was keen to get home and have an early night.

However much they talked about needing to know who had bought Mrs Danson's stick, they were no nearer to thinking of a way to find out.

After tea on Thursday, Mr and Mrs Pleeth and both the children were relaxing in the sitting room - Mrs Pleeth with her knitting and the others with their books - when a knock sounded at the back door. Mrs Pleeth went to answer it. Reverend Ross followed her back into the sitting room. He greeted Mr Pleeth and everyone, and accepted an invitation to sit down.

"I've just come with the latest edition of the parish magazine," Reverend Ross explained. He held out a single sheet of flimsy paper, typed and home-printed in violet ink. "I'm hoping to encourage as many people as possible to come to the fête on The Common on August Bank Holiday Monday, that's August the 7th."

"I shall certainly be there, Reverend. I'll be helping in the tea tent," Mrs Pleeth said.

"We're very grateful for all the assistance we can get to man the stalls. Miss Nicholls is usually such a help, but she's so busy looking after her mother at the moment, I doubt she'll be able to spare the time this year."

"How is Mrs Danson?" Mrs Pleeth enquired.

"Not good, I'm afraid. I'm quite worried about her. I know Miss Nicholls is very concerned."

"We'll go to the fête," Megan said. "Well, at least I will. John will have to go to work."

"I think Mr Fairbrother will give John the day off for the Bank Holiday," Reverend Ross assured her.

"I shall be on duty that day," Mr Pleeth explained, "but, of course, that gives me the perfect excuse to visit every stall. Must make sure there are no breaches of the peace on The Common on the big day." He laughed.

There was another tap at the back door, but before Mrs Pleeth could reach it, the door opened and Miss Nicholls stepped into the kitchen. She looked white-faced and anxious.

"Mr Pleeth, so sorry to trouble you. I wondered if you could make a phone call for me, please. Reverend, I'm so pleased I've found you. I went to the Rectory and Mrs Judd said you may be here."

"Dear lady," said Reverend Ross, rising from his seat and stepping forward to take Miss Nicholls' hand, "whatever is the matter?"

"It's my mother, Reverend." Miss Nicholls hesitated. "She's just . . . passed away."

CHAPTER 39

Miss Nicholls looked so pale that Megan was afraid she might faint. Reverend Ross took a firm hold on her arm and steered her into an armchair. She rested her head against the back of the chair and closed her eyes.

Mrs Pleeth headed out into the kitchen and Megan could hear her putting the kettle on.

Nobody spoke for a moment, but all eyes were on Miss Nicholls. Her chest heaved and it looked as if she was choking back sobs. Megan hated to see Miss Nicholls so upset. But, of course, her mother had just died, so she would be.

Another death in the village, so quickly on the heels of the last two, who had died so horribly. Oh, goodness! Megan's brain worked overtime. What had Mrs Danson died of?

As though she had read Megan's mind, Miss Nicholls opened her eyes. With head bowed, she spoke quietly to Reverend Ross, but they could all hear.

"She had a heart attack. It was not entirely unexpected. She had suffered from a weak heart for some time and she had been very poorly for the past couple of weeks, as you know. I'm so sorry to be such a nuisance. I feel I've quite forgotten my manners. Didn't mean to burst in and . . ." she clutched her handkerchief to her mouth.

"Nonsense, Miss Nicholls. You did exactly the right thing to come and find me. I'm glad Mrs Judd suggested it. And I'm sure Mr and Mrs Pleeth will do anything they can to help in such tragic circumstances."

Miss Nicholls turned to Mr Pleeth. "Could you possibly telephone the doctor for me, please?" She produced a slip of paper from her pocket. "And I need to let my aunt know. Miss Elsie Danson. She lives at Eastbourne, on the south coast. She really should be notified."

Mr Pleeth got up and took the paper from Miss Nicholls.

"I'll see to it right away, Miss Nicholls."

He went off up the passageway to his police office where the telephone was. Megan heard the door close behind him.

She felt so sorry for Miss Nicholls. She wanted to do something to help, but she couldn't think of anything. If she started trying to join in the conversation, it would only make matters worse.

She had a sudden thought. She leaned over and whispered to John: "Can I go into your room?"

John nodded.

Megan got up and slipped out of the room and ran upstairs. She went into her brother's room and opened the wardrobe and pulled out the sack stuffed at the back. The string binding the saw on to the walking stick was wound round tight but she managed to get it off. She put the saw back with the magnet and replaced the sack in the back of John's wardrobe.

She looked at the '*E.D.*' engraved in curly letters on the silver knob of the walking stick. Miss Nicholls thought her mother had sold her walking stick. Megan had heard Mrs Danson tell her that. So it would be a welcome surprise to have it back. She headed downstairs.

Mrs Pleeth was going round the sitting room handing out cups of tea. Miss Nicholls was sitting forward in her chair now. Megan went straight to her and handed her the stick and then went back to her seat beside John.

Miss Nicholls gazed at the stick in disbelief. What little colour had come back into her face drained away until she was even paler than before. Her eyes were wide and staring, her voice hardly above a whisper as she looked at Megan.

"Where did you get this?"

Before Megan could answer, Mr Pleeth came back into the room.

"I've spoken to the doctor in Market Hampton, Miss Nicholls. He'll come out right away to issue the death certificate. And I've spoken to your aunt. Miss Danson sends her deepest condolences on your loss and will be writing to you directly."

Miss Nicholls appeared not to have heard him. She neither looked at him nor spoke to him. All her attention was on the walking stick. She held it close to her body and wrapped her arms round it, as though it was a person. She rocked back and forth in her chair, tears running down her cheeks.

"This belonged to my father," she whispered. "After his death, my mother had it cut down so that she could use it. They had the same initials. Funny coincidence . . . He was, properly speaking, my stepfather. My own father was killed in the first war when I was only a baby. I don't remember him at all. My mother remarried. Ernest Danson was the only father I ever knew, and he meant the world to me.

"He died in the Battersea Park rail disaster, a couple of years before the war. We lived in the London suburbs then and I taught in the local school. My father worked in Central London, near Victoria Station. Sometimes he would arrange to take an afternoon off from his office. My mother would travel up to town with him on his usual train. He had to be at the office for 9 o'clock but he always liked to be early. My mother would spend the morning shopping along Oxford Street. They would meet at Selfridges for lunch and go to a matinée at the theatre in the afternoon and be home around six."

Miss Nicholls paused to mop her eyes. She took a sip of tea and continued.

"That's what they were going to do that day. It was April the 2nd. I'll never forget it. They had tickets for 'On Your Toes'. It was a new musical that had not long opened, to very good reviews. They were so looking forward to it.

"But the train never got to Victoria Station. There was a signal failure and the train behind ran into the back of theirs. My father was killed outright and my mother was terribly injured. She never walked again.

"When she recovered enough to come home, we decided we'd had enough of London life. I applied for teaching-posts in country areas and we were delighted when I was accepted here in Bartlemere. We loved moving into our cottage and we were so happy there until . . . Where did you get this from, Megan?"

"I . . . er . . . found it, Miss Nicholls. Down by The Mere." She couldn't possibly tell the whole truth. She crossed her fingers that what she had said would be enough.

Miss Nicholls stared at her with the most strange expression on her face. Megan knew Miss Nicholls didn't believe her. What else could she say? She couldn't explain the whole story.

"Miss Nicholls, your mother told you she'd sold it, didn't she? I was near your cottage one day and I heard her say that. The person she sold it to must have lost it. I thought you'd like to have it back."

"I can't tell you how glad I am to have it back, Megan. But my mother didn't sell it, despite what you heard her say. She gave it away. And I very much doubt the person she gave it to lost it."

"Who did she give it to?"

"Cyril Roseby."

CHAPTER 40

"But she couldn't have!" Megan protested.

It made no sense. The owner of the stick had sawn through the chain. If Mr Roseby had done it he would have known the chain was likely to give way, and he would never have climbed up on the ducking stool that night.

"Megan! Don't contradict, it's rude!" Reverend Ross looked shocked at Megan talking back to Miss Nicholls. "There is no reason at all why Mrs Danson shouldn't have made a present of the stick to her friend Mr Roseby."

"Friend? Friend?" Miss Nicholls nearly shouted the word. It seemed to catch in her throat and came out as an ugly, twisted sound. "That monster Roseby was no friend to my mother. He was a leech, a bloodsucker, he drained her dry!"

Reverend Ross sat with a stunned expression on his face, quite taken aback by Miss Nicholls' outburst.

Miss Nicholls' face now was red and burning. She seemed a different woman from the one who had stumbled into the room so shortly before, needing to be revived with tea.

"I made a mistake," she announced, firmly. "I did a foolish and wrong thing, and Roseby found out about it. He went to my mother and told her that unless she did exactly as he told her, he would expose me and what I had done, and my mother and I would lose everything."

There was a shocked silence throughout the room that seemed to last for ever. Then Mrs Pleeth's teacup clinked as she replaced it in its saucer. It broke the moment.

"But that's blackmail," Reverend Ross protested.

"Yes," Miss Nicholls agreed. She had regained her self-control and spoke more calmly now. "Blackmail is exactly what Cyril Roseby was up to. And I never knew a thing about it until the early hours of this morning, when my mother – who knew she didn't have much time left – told me the whole story.

"A couple of weeks ago, Megan, you may well have heard my mother telling me that she had been selling our family treasures. The truth was that Roseby had demanded these things from her. He would come to our house two or three times a week and pick out what he wanted and she handed them over to him, one after another, in the hope of buying his silence.

"But of course, vermin like him never give up. The more she gave him, the more he asked for. He began forcing her to go with him to Market Hampton on the first of each month, the day her pension was paid into her bank account. He made her draw out money and give it to him. There was no end to his greed. He was a foul man and he made my mother's life a misery."

Miss Nicholls turned to Reverend Ross:

"When you spoke up for him that Sunday in church, I knew nothing of all this but my mother was deeply distressed. In fact, she was ill with worry at the time, and it brought on her heart symptoms."

"My dear Miss Nicholls, I had no idea. I can't begin to tell you how sorry. . ."

Miss Nicholls cut off his apology: "I know you said it with the best of intentions. You were in ignorance of the truth, as much as I was. You tried to see good in a man who, in all honesty, had very little good about him."

Miss Nicholls lapsed into silence. Everyone in the room sat perfectly still, too tense to move, still unable to believe what they had heard.

Miss Nicholls turned back to Megan: "Please tell me, Megan. Where exactly was my mother's stick when you found it?"

John got up from his chair and went to stand beside Megan.

"I'll explain," he said. "We were looking for something we thought had fallen in The Mere. We were fishing about and we dredged up your mother's stick. It was stuck in the reeds under the big sycamore tree, near the ducking stool."

"Why did you think it might be there?" Miss Nicholls seemed astonished.

"Oh, no, we weren't looking for it. We found it by accident. It was . . ."

"It was what?"

"Well, it was attached to something else."

"And what was that?"

"If you'll excuse me a minute, I'll show you."

John left the room and Megan could hear him running up the stairs. A few moments later he came down with the sack and emptied the contents on to the sitting room floor. All the adults stared in amazement at the chain and the saw and the magnet.

"What was the stick fixed to?"

"This!" John held up the saw. The string round its handle was still curled, where it had been bound tightly round the walking stick.

"Let me get this right." Mr Pleeth joined in the conversation. "You got this saw and Mrs Danson's stick out of The Mere, and they were tied together."

"Yes."

"How did you get them out?" Reverend Ross wanted to know.

"With the magnet. We'd put the magnet in the water and the saw stuck to it and the stick came out with it."

"Wait a minute." Mr Pleeth was trying to piece things together. "Why were you putting the magnet in The Mere in the first place?"

"We were trying to fish something out of the water."

"What?"

Megan and John glanced at one another. Megan shrugged.

"The saw." John said.

CHAPTER 41

Mr Pleeth reached forward and took the saw. He held it up and looked at it closely. Reverend Ross, meanwhile, had picked up the chain from the carpet and was studying it carefully, especially the broken link. Mr Pleeth saw what he was doing. He gestured to Reverend Ross, who passed the chain across to him.

"This saw," Mr Pleeth said, "has a blade for cutting metal. This chain's made of metal and it's been cut through. Is there anything you want to tell me about that, John?"

Before John could answer, Reverend Ross spoke again:

"I can remember, John, the first time we had a session of looking through the microscope, you brought some metal fragments. We examined them together and I told you I thought it was swarf – the cast off from metal that had been sawn through." He paused.

"That's right." John nodded.

"I never asked you, but I'm asking now. Where did you get that swarf?"

"I picked it up on the evening of Mr Roseby's accident, by the iron hoop where the ducking stool used to be anchored down. The chain was missing. Everybody assumed the chain or the padlock had broken and that's why the ducking stool fell down. I just went out to have a look round, because I thought there might be something interesting to see there. When I found the swarf I didn't know what it was. That's why I brought it to look at under your microscope. I didn't even know what swarf was until you told me."

"But you soon put two and two together, eh, and guessed that the chain had been sabotaged?"

"Yes."

"Where did you find the chain?" Mr Pleeth asked.

"It was caught in the willow tree on the opposite side of the The Mere."

"What made you look there?"

"I used maths to work out the likely trajectory, if the chain was thrown in the air when the ducking stool went down."

Mr Pleeth shook his head in disbelief. "Reckon I could do with you working alongside o' me, if you can do that kind of thing. It'd make my life a lot easier."

Miss Nicholls hadn't taken her eyes off Megan all the time John was giving his explanation.

"I need to ask you something else," she said. "Have I understood this right? You think whoever had my mother's stick tied the saw onto it and used it to cut through the chain so that the ducking stool went down into the water when Mr Roseby climbed on it?"

"Yes," Megan answered straight away. "So Mr Roseby couldn't have been the one who did it. That's why I contradicted you. I'm sorry. I didn't mean to be rude then."

Miss Nicholls took a deep breath and sat back in the chair once more.

"That's all right, Megan. I understand. I think you and your brother know a lot more about all this than any of the rest of us."

Megan and John stood side by side, saying nothing.

Mrs Pleeth cleared her throat.

"May I ask a question, please?"

Everyone turned to look at her.

"I don't like to pry, Miss Nicholls, but I wondered if you would feel able to tell us what this secret was that Mr Roseby was using to blackmail your mother with?"

Miss Nicholls gave a little humourless laugh.

"I might as well. There can be no more secrets now. I followed my heart instead of my head. My young man was in the R.A.F., Pilot Officer James Beverley. Jim was a fine young man and I was in love, I admit it. Eighteen months ago we heard that he was to be sent behind enemy lines on a very dangerous mission. We knew how risky it was. He could easily be killed. He had forty-eight hours leave before he went. We knew it might be the last time we'd ever be together. So we got a special licence and we got married in secret. We didn't tell anyone, not even my mother.

"I know it was a rash thing to do, but when there's a war on, anything can happen. We said goodbye and Jim went off on his mission. Then I learned that he and his crew hadn't made it back. He was missing, presumed dead. A long time later I heard that he was still alive. He'd been captured, and ever since then he's been a prisoner of war. I'm just thankful for that, although it may be years before we see each other again."

Megan sat listening in amazement to Miss Nicholls' story.

"The trouble began when Roseby came to the village last year. He'd met my Jim in a transit camp as Jim was preparing to leave on his mission. Jim told Roseby about our secret wedding and he also let it slip that I was a teacher. Roseby tracked us down. He went to my mother and told her that I was now a married woman. You can imagine how shocked my mother was. I'd done it behind her back, of course, and worse still, I'd put my whole career at risk. If the authorities knew I was no longer single, then I'd lose my job, and we'd have to leave the cottage, and where would we both live? I wouldn't be able to get another teaching post.

"So my poor mother was easy prey to this evil man, who traded on her fears and her love for me and her disappointment that I'd done something so foolish. So she was paying Roseby off, and keeping from me that she knew my secret. You can imagine how it preyed on her mind. It took a heavy toll of her."

"Poor lady," Mrs Pleeth murmured.

"That's not the last of it. When that rat, Roseby, had got everything he could from my mother, he came to me. All the valuables in our home belonged to my mother. I didn't have anything except my salary. But he started demanding money. He came into the school one Saturday evening when I'd gone to put up some displays of the children's work, ready for Monday morning. He said he knew all about me and Beverley, and if I didn't give him money he would report me."

Megan couldn't believe her ears.

"We overheard that conversation, Miss Nicholls. It was the day we arrived back in Bartlemere. We walked past the school with our mother. We thought you were rehearsing for the play."

"I remember you telling me about that, Megan," Reverend Ross said, "because I was surprised they were rehearsing at the school when we usually rehearsed at the Rectory."

"That was the day you told us about Tiger and the cream cake."

CHAPTER 42

"Excuse me, Miss Nicholls," John butted in. "Did you say your mother went into Market Hampton on the first of each month?"

"That's right. Her pension day at the bank."

"Will you excuse me a moment, please?"

John left the room and Megan heard him running up the stairs. He was back in an instant. He put a piece of paper into Miss Nicholls' hands.

"This was posted in Market Hampton on the first of May. Do you recognise that handwriting, Miss Nicholls?"

"Yes. It's my mother's. She obviously sent something to Mr Hains. I don't know what it was. Is it important?"

"It might be."

"Did your mother ever bring anything back for tea when she went to Market Hampton with Mr Roseby?" Megan asked.

"Occasionally. She liked cream cakes. She might bring some back. Not that the cream was ever very nice. Mock cream, you know, while the war's on. Why are you asking these strange questions, children?"

Megan didn't know what to say. They had already said too much. But how could they stop now. The lid had been taken off Pandora's box and it was impossible to put it back on.

"Reverend Ross, you said Mrs Danson used to sit in her wheelchair near the ducking stool two or three mornings a week."

"That's right, Megan. Mr Roseby used to wheel her there and tuck her rug round her and she would sit there until you came to take her home at lunchtime, right Miss Nicholls?"

"Yes."

"How long was she there?"

"An hour or two. She would take a book. Or just sit and look at the view."

John cleared his throat. Megan knew exactly what he was thinking. She wondered what he was going to say.

"Mr Pleeth," John began, "this is awfully difficult to say, but I've got to say it. I think you should ask Miss Nicholls whether she is sure her mother gave her walking stick away."

Mr Pleeth looked at John very seriously. Megan held her breath. Then Mr Pleeth turned to Miss Nicholls:

"Do you know for sure that your mother gave her walking stick away?"

"She told me Roseby had everything."

"But the walking stick in particular?"

"Er . . . no, perhaps she didn't mention it specifically. Why?"

Mr Pleeth looked to John to answer. In response, John walked over to Miss Nicholls and gently took the walking stick from her hands. He picked up the saw and wound the string back round the bottom of the walking stick, then he put the saw down with the blade between the broken ends of the chain. Without a word he stepped back and stood beside Megan.

196

Miss Nicholls' eyes followed his every move. As he stepped back, she gave a gasp and covered her face with her hands.

Mrs Pleeth did the same as she realised the significance of what John had done. Reverend Ross made a little rumbling noise in his throat and shook his head. Mr Pleeth looked at John and nodded his head sadly.

"I think you've about summed up what happened, my lad." Mr Pleeth got up and walked over to John. Mrs Pleeth left her seat and went into the kitchen, obviously thinking it was time for another cup of tea.

Reverend Ross spoke softly to Miss Nicholls: "I think your mother may have decided to find a way to deal with her persecutor."

Mr Pleeth took up the story.

"She must have fastened the saw to the end of her stick. It would have taken her a long while, but every time she sat in her chair by the ducking stool, little by little she sawed a bit further through the chain, keeping the saw covered with her rug. And when she'd finished, she threw the stick and saw into The Mere."

He looked at John: "Is that what you think?

John nodded.

"What was that business with Mrs Danson's handwriting about?" Mr Pleeth asked.

John looked uncomfortable but he gave his answer.

"That was the wrapping paper off the parcel bomb that killed Mr Hains."

"What?" Miss Nicholls was horrified. "You said that parcel was post-marked last May. And anyway, why on earth would my mother send Mr Hains a parcel bomb?"

John produced the other piece of wrapping paper. "The parcel was lost in the post for ages. It went all over the country before it was delivered to Mr Hains. And it was actually addressed to Mr Roseby. Look."

John handed the piece of paper to Mr Pleeth who read it and passed it on to Miss Nicholls.

"It's true," he said. "Where did you get this, John?"

"Megan found it on The Common."

"So, let me understand what you're suggesting." Once more, Mr Pleeth was putting the facts in order. "You think before she sawed through the chain, Mrs Danson tried to blow Mr Roseby up with a parcel bomb!"

"Yes. And . . ."

"For goodness sake, don't tell me there's any more!" Miss Nicholls exclaimed.

Just then, Mrs Pleeth came through with the fresh pot of tea.

"Good timing, Marjorie," Mr Pleeth remarked, as he took the tray from her and put it on the side table. Mrs Pleeth poured out and everyone accepted another cup.

"If there is more, I need to hear it," Miss Nicholls said, pulling herself together.

Megan took over the story.

"Reverend Ross told us that Mr Roseby brought a cream cake to the Rectory."

"It was a rum baba, actually," Reverend Ross interrupted, "with a very strong rum flavour, as I recall. He said someone had given it to him, but he didn't like rum, so he offered it to me."

"That would have been around the first of June," Megan pressed on. "Tiger, the Rectory cat, licked some of the cream off the cake. He knocked it on the floor so, fortunately Reverend Ross didn't eat it. Because the cream was poisoned."

"Or so we think," John added.

"Good gracious, is that what did it for poor old Tiger, that rum baba?" Reverend Ross found it hard to take all this in.

"We think maybe Mrs Danson brought it back from Market Hampton and gave it to Mr Roseby." There, Megan had said it. It was a dreadful accusation, but it was what they truly believed had happened.

"After she had added poison to it?" Mr Pleeth asked.

Megan nodded. She couldn't say it out loud.

Miss Nicholls flopped back in her chair. She had nothing left to say. She was exhausted.

"Poor lady," Mrs Pleeth commented quietly. "She must have been so desperate under Roseby's threats that she lost her senses. She would never have done such things in her right mind."

Megan thought of the rules that Mr Pleeth had quoted, at the time of Mr Martin's arrest: 'Such a disease of the mind that she did not know that what she was doing was wrong.'

She had liked Mrs Danson and admired her. She really hadn't known her at all.

Reverend Ross was looking with concern at Miss Nicholls, who seemed unable to gather her thoughts.

"Dear lady," he said quietly, "there is one thing I can tell you that may ease your mind. I was reading in the paper about the new Education Act. It has passed through parliament and next week the King will sign his assent to make it law. In future, women teachers will be allowed to marry, so you need have no fear that you will lose your post. And I am sure I speak for us all when I say I hope that you will stay at Bartlemere school for many years to come."

Miss Nicholls looked at him, but was unable to find words.

"And the school leaving age is to be raised to sixteen, so you, young John, will be able to resume your studies."

"That's good," John replied.

Mrs Pleeth stood up: "This has been a very difficult evening for everybody. We can't do anything about the funeral until the morning. I'm sure Reverend Ross will help with all the arrangements, won't you?"

"Yes, yes of course. My pleasure."

"Miss Nicholls, after the doctor has been, if you would like to come back and stay here with us, you are most welcome. It won't take me a minute to make up a bed."

"Yes, please. I'd be grateful. If you're sure it's no trouble."

Reverend Ross stood up: "I'll walk back with you to your place, Miss Nicholls, and wait with you until the doctor comes."

"Thank you. I'd appreciate that."

"Walter, don't you have to go out and check the village blackout?"

"I do indeed. I'll get my helmet."

"And you two, off to bed. See you in the morning. Goodnight."

"Goodnight, Mrs Pleeth. Goodnight everybody."

John reached out his hand and Megan took it. He squeezed her hand and led her out of the sitting room and up the stairs.

"You were great, Meg. Well done."

"You too, John. Great."

They gave each other a hug on the landing, before they wished one another a last goodnight and went wearily to bed.

CHAPTER 43

Monday 31ˢᵗ July
Dearest Mummy
It was Mrs Danson's funeral today. Everyone came to the church. It was very sad.
Miss Nicholls cried a lot. I wore my Sunday best frock and my black patent shoes.
They pinch my toes a bit now. Mrs Fairbrother's cat, Misty, at the farm has had
kittens. We can't see them yet because they are too little. She had them in the
barn. We can go and see them when their eyes are open. Mrs Fairbrother is going
to ask Reverend Ross if he wants one. I really hope he does because he likes cats
and he misses Tiger. I asked Mrs Pleeth if we could have one but she said not
because Mr Pleeth doesn't like cats. She said they make him sneeze. I expect he
wouldn't like cat fur on his uniform either. I have written too much and John will
have to write very small. Love you loads and loads and loads.
Megan x x x x x

THE END